IMAGINE

Imagine a group of keen writers –
a group that has existed since 2015.

Imagine the members of that group
pooling talents, skills and
inspirations to produce a collection
of short stories and a few poems.

Imagine that book is in your hand
right now.

Just IMAGINE

i

IMAGINE

First edition published 2023

© *WiSE - Writers in Stannington and Ecclesfield 2023*

ISBN: 9798858431183

Imprint: Independently published

Also by the group

As Stannington Library Writers Group

1Stannthology	2016
NxStannthology	2017
LateStannthology	2018

As Ecclesfield Library Writers Group:

Tales from the Library	2017
Time for More Tales	2019

Joint production:

Christmas Anthology	2017

As WiSE – Writers in Stannington and Ecclesfield

Splash!	2019
Zoom Out	2020
One Way Ticket	2021
And The Winner Is …	2021
Words from the Wise	2021
15 Writers in Worlds of their Own	2022

All the above titles are available through amazon.co.uk

CONTENTS

Writers featured in this anthology   **viii**
Preface   **xiii**

THE STORIES

The Mad Bishop and Bear	Penny Wragg	**1**
Any News of George	Jean Atherton	**9**
Lost and Found	Ken Hutton	**13**
A Very Serious Conversation	Bob Mynors	**25**
Shades of Lapis Blue	Graham Bloodworth	**35**
The Wedding Do	P Wright	**41**
Ghost Haiku	Diane Bingham	**59**
Cake and Coronets	Sue Allott	**63**
As If … If Only	Jacqueline Blackburn	**67**
All Dead All Gone	Bob Mynors	**77**
The Silent Man	Neil McGill	**93**
A New World Order	Annette Phillips	**129**
New Springs	Penny Wragg	**137**
The Mayor, Her Lover, His Wife and the Rat	Glen Fryer	**145**
How Is It?	Ken Hutton	**194**

Filling in the Gaps in the History Books	Bob Mynors	**197**
Freddie the Fox's Ordeal	Sue Allott	**201**
Two Weeks Off	P Wright	**217**
Lost and Found	Jean Atherton	**223**
Herod Was Completely Misunderstood	Annette Phillips	**233**
Fly-by-Night Email	Bob Mynors	**240**
Warehouse	Graham Bloodworth	**243**
The Dance-Off	Sue Allott	**255**
Father's Day	Annette Phillips	**272**
The Election Trap	Bob Mynors	**275**
The Garden Centre	P Wright	**283**
The Stone House Remembered	Sue Allott	**290**
Every Witch Should Have a Black Cat	Jean Atherton	**297**
If Only …	Penny Wragg	**307**
Desert Island Discs	Bob Mynors	**311**

Writers featured in this anthology

PENNY WRAGG

Brought up in Millhouses but a Stannington resident for over forty years, Penny has always loved writing. Her first published work was in her junior school magazine: a poem about a wizard. She has since written poetry, memoir and, under the influence of this group, murder stories! If stranded on a desert island she would ask for an unlimited supply of pens and paper!

JEAN ATHERTON

Jean was born and raised in South Yorkshire, and still lives in the town where she was born. Now a mother and a grandmother, she has always spent a great deal of her time surrounded by family. Only in later years did Jean find the time and the motivation to start writing. Now she enjoys creating short stories and poetry, whether humorous or deeply, darkly serious.

KEN HUTTON

Born and brought up in Edinburgh, Ken lived and worked in various locations before settling in Sheffield where he has lived for forty years. Retiring after a long career in social services, he found himself at a loose end and began writing stories for his grandchildren, self-publishing his first in 2020. Writing can be a solitary enterprise but Ken has found support, advice and companionship as a member of WiSE.

BOB MYNORS

Bob has six entries in this year's anthology: is this a record? They range from a fictionalised family history to a fantastical imagining of a much-loved radio classic, and even include a rare poetic effort. Some of these stories result from painstaking and back-breaking effort and research, whilst others are thrown together as the tyranny of the deadline bears down. All, he claims, were great fun to write though.

GRAHAM BLOODWORTH

Born in 1959 in Worksop, Nottinghamshire, Graham spent time on various RAF bases as his father plied his trade as an aircraft electrical technician. Moving to Sheffield in 1968, he is best remembered for working in the toy and model store, Beatties of London Ltd. With a strong interest in science fiction and science fantasy, he is a self-published author.

PAMELA WRIGHT

Pamela has always wanted to write, and she is also an avid reader. Especially, she wants to write books that contain a little humour. She feels that being part of Ecclesfield Library Writers Group is helping her grow and develop as a writer all the time. Much of this she attributes to the experiences she shares at meetings with fellow group members.

DIANE BINGHAM

Diane is interested in family and social history research and the origins and development of language. Haiku is a popular Japanese poetic form of three short lines of 5, 7 and 5 syllables. Within these restrictions, the aim is to convey a moment of insight from something observed.

SUE ALLOTT

Sue Allott has lived in Stannington since 1992 after marrying husband George. She's always been interested in the English language and found an opportunity in 2016 to further this interest, when she was encouraged to join the writing group at the library. She finds writing therapeutic and hard work, but enjoys sharing her love of storytelling with everyone satisfying. Her main inspirations come from nature's creatures, colours, fauna and people and finds there's always something out there to write about.

JACQUELINE BLACKBURN

Jacqueline came to Sheffield to study English Literature then, ten years ago, began embarked on Creative Writing courses with the OU, gaining an MA in 2019. To date she has focused on short stories and is now keen to explore the long-term effects of Covid on people's lives in her writing. She joined the group to exchange ideas and cakes with fellow writers.

NEIL McGILL

Raised within an Irish heritage in a South Yorkshire mining village, Neil is one of four siblings. Leaving school with modest qualifications, he entered the engineering industry as an apprentice fabricator. After studying engineering, management and education at local colleges, he has become a lecturer in engineering. An optimist, he supports Barnsley Football Club, and also enjoys music and driving.

ANNETTE PHILLIPS

A newcomer to the writers' group, Annette has always loved books and has enjoyed creative writing, first as a mature student at Sheffield Hallam University. She has written poetry, prose and memoir over the years. Originally from Devon, she has lived in Sheffield for 35 years. Art and the countryside are her other passions, as well as a liking for a friendly pint in a pub.

GLEN FRYER

Glen has lived in Sheffield for the best part of fifty years, but she started life in Liverpool where she learned most of her wit. With her wits about her, she joined the group six years ago and is still just a keen member of the group, having written endless short stories and three novels along the way.

WiSE – Writers in Stannington and Ecclesfield presents another collection of short works, mostly prose fiction but featuring some poetry and biography too. Much of the work in this volume was created for the group's monthly meetings in Ecclesfield and in Stannington, though some have been specifically created for inclusion.

If you wish to pass comment on any of our offerings, whether negative or positive, we would like to see them. Please send them to wisewritersgroup@gmail.com. Use the same email address if you are interested in attending a meeting and possibly becoming a member of the group.

The Mad Bishop and Bear

Penny Wragg

Your average church congregation doesn't usually welcome bears to their services. Paddington had got off on the wrong foot at St Hugh's when he offered the priest some marmalade to make the communion bread tastier. The curate had chased him out of the building. Mrs Bird had to miss the rest of the service to go after him. Luckily, she forgave him. She had a very soft spot for the little bear. She made a mental note to write to the PCC at St Hugh's concerning inclusivity.

Mr and Mrs Brown suggested St Michael's as a family-friendly church and Paddington was adored by all the children there. They had all taken to wearing duffle coats, even in summer! Such was his charisma as a style icon.

One Sunday, a bishop came to conduct a confirmation service. Paddington knew that a bishop was a very important man in the church hierarchy. He had met one before and struck up an instant rapport, asking him if he could try on his special hat. He later learned that it was called a mitre. He offered to swap hats with the bishop, but the bishop just smiled at him and patted him on the head.

"Bless you, little bear," he said.

Today this was a different bishop who he hadn't seen before. Or had he? He looked again. Underneath the posh robes and mitre, the face was familiar. This was someone he recognised. A frisson of fear made his fur stand on end. The bishop's eyes met his. He instantly looked shocked and then slowly his mouth curled into a sneer. All the way through reciting the Creed, he looked at the little bear. Paddington gave him a very hard stare. It was Mr Buchanan! But how could it be Mr Buchanan? He was in prison. How had he escaped?

As soon as the service was over and the bishop's procession had processed, as it does, to the vestry, Paddington left his seat.

"Won't be long," he whispered to Judy Brown.

"Paddington, where are you going? Wait…."

Paddington had gone in pursuit of the bishop or the "pretend bishop" as he named him in his head.

Phoenix Buchanan had been extremely surprised and annoyed to see Paddington Bear in the congregation at St Michael's. He had no idea he was a church-going bear. Damn it! The observant bear had recognised him, despite his lovingly crafted outfit of bishop's robes and mitre. He was not going to interfere with his plans again. He had gone to a great deal of trouble to manage his escape from prison, helped by several of his fellow inmates. He had bribed them with a promise of a postal delivery of new costumes for their latest theatrical production *Les Misérables* and some cupcakes for their regular afternoon teas. Of course, he wouldn't bother now he was out. No more Mr Nice Guy! It went against the grain. Phoenix Buchanan was known as a nasty piece of work, and he intended it to stay that way.

His disguise as a bishop had worked perfectly. The real visiting bishop had been diverted to an isolation cell and locked in. Buchanan had got his own outfit which Fats and Smelly had hidden in the laundry. He then proceeded to a meeting with the prison chaplain dispensing a few "Bless you" greetings on the way. Utilising his excellent acting skills, he made some brief recommendations on spiritual support in the prison to a bemused chaplain and left by the main gate. *Easy peasy!*

His first plan now was to steal some items from the treasury at St Michael's. Over the years he had acquired knowledge from several criminal contacts and he knew that the 17th century chalice and paten were the most valuable items in it. He had a buyer lined up already. That nosey little bear was not going to stop him. He ran down the steps to the treasury with the key, looking behind to make sure he wasn't being followed.

Paddington had found a nice little hidey hole, just the right size for a bear but too small for a human. It was fortunate that he had joined the Sunday school church tour only two weeks ago and discovered all the nooks and crannies in the old building unknown to many adults. He would wait for Mr Buchanan to come back up the stairs. He realised that he hadn't thought his plan through beyond that point. He got his mobile phone out of his duffle coat pocket and sent a text to both Judy and Jonathan in case one of them missed it.

Phoenix Buchanan held the gleaming chalice and paten in his hands. Wow, they were quite something! He wrapped them in the spare altar cloth which he had taken with him and set off back up the steps. Several things happened in quick succession.

Paddington jumped down the top two steps and Buchanan tripped over him and fell backwards with a shriek, dropping his treasures on the way. Unfortunately, Paddington also lost his footing and tumbled down the steps, landing on top of our bogus bishop.

"Aah………!" yelled Paddington.

This is where Reverend Grantham, the vicar of St Michael's, comes into our story. Up until now a background figure, he becomes a hero. He had spotted Paddington heading to the little hidey hole and followed at a distance, watching events unfold with interest. He now comes into his own.

"What on earth are you doing, Bishop?" says he, surveying the crumpled heap which is Phoenix Buchanan.

"He's not a real bishop, your Reverence," Paddington interjected. "He's a failed actor and escaped prisoner."

"Well really!" exclaimed the vicar and hit Buchanan over the head with a conveniently situated and extremely heavy leather-bound volume of the Bible.

"I thought Christianity was all about peace and goodwill and forgiveness, vicar," said Paddington quietly.

"Well, you see, Paddington, there's a time and a place and it's not now and it's not here."

"Fair enough, vicar."

Judy and Jonathan had followed Paddington's instructions and telephoned the police who were waiting outside the main door of the church. Other members of the congregation were guarding all the other exits, just in case. They all cheered Paddington and the vicar as they came out. When they saw Phoenix Buchanan, they all booed loudly.

"It reminds me of my days as a pantomime villain." He grinned ruefully.

Everyone waved bye-bye to him as he was bundled into a police car, but not before Paddington had given him a very hard stare.

"Well done, Paddington!" said Mr Brown.

"You're such a brave little bear!" said Mrs Bird.

Revd Grantham cleared his throat.

"I'd just like to make an announcement, everyone. In honour of our great friend Paddington Bear, from next Sunday we are going to have breakfast before the 10.30 service. What shall we have to eat?"

And everyone chorused, "Marmalade sandwiches!"

Author's note

The prompt for our stories was to write about a pub sign.

'The Mad Bishop and Bear' is the name of a pub in Paddington, London. 'Bear' is of course in honour of Paddington.

'The mad bishop' was a bishop who sold land to the railway at a ridiculously low price, so everyone thought that he was mad.

Is There Any News on George?

Jean Atherton

"Is there any news on George?" Eva shouted from the allotment next to Edward's.

Edward looked up from his newspaper.

"I spoke to his wife yesterday. She said it looks as though he'll be able to come home this weekend," Edward replied.

Eva moved closer to the privet hedge which separated their allotments. "If you happen to be in touch with him, or his wife, give them my best wishes please, Edward."

"No problem," he replied as he raised the newspaper back to reading position. Edward and George had known each other since school and remained good friends throughout their adult years.

They had applied for an allotment and were pleased when they were allocated one at the side of each other. They helped each other prepare the ground ready to grow their favourite veggies.

Edward was a portly, jovial man. His cheeks puffy and red, weathered by the outdoors, "Due to all the gardening in the allotment," he laughed as his pal commented on his high colour.

George, on the other hand, was completely opposite. He was tall, slender, and paler in colour. They spent every day in the allotments. Their wives would do a packed lunch with a bit of chocolate for afters. Edward had a camping stove in his shed along with tea bags and coffee, each day George supplied the fresh milk. Their friendship worked well and they were very close.

When George was rushed into hospital with a heart attack, Edward was devastated. He waited a few days before ringing Mary, George's wife.

"Edward, could you keep an eye on the allotment for George please? I will come up to see you in a few days."

"Don't worry about the allotment Mary. There's not much to do so I'll keep things running. Just keep me updated with George's recovery."

"Will do. Thanks Edward."

That was over a week ago and no update from Mary.

Edward had made himself a cup of tea and was relaxing on his bench when he felt someone beside him.

"George, how good to see you. I've really missed you. How are you feeling now? Don't worry about doing any weeding, Eva and I have been keeping your allotment tidy. So good to see you, I'll make you a cuppa."

Edward was so excited to see his best friend he couldn't stop talking, "Just be a mo., George." With that Edward disappeared into his shed. Minutes later he appeared with a steaming hot mug of tea. George was no longer there.

"Wonder where he went to," Edward muttered as he sat down to finish his cuppa.

"Hello, you must be Edward. My Dad talked about you a lot."

Edward looked up at a very distinguished gent who had a look of his friend, George.

"I'm George's son. My mother asked me to come and let you know the sad news. We lost Dad last night. He was getting ready to come home but suffered a massive heart attack."

Edward's mouth dropped open. He wondered what had just happened. Had he fallen asleep? Had he been dreaming? He looked down at the steaming mug of tea. A tear ran down his cheek and dropped off his chin.

LOST AND FOUND

Ken Hutton

Jean had been a looker in her day but, despite all the attention, she never seemed able to make a go of it with even the most eligible of suitors. For most of her career, she had been a fitness instructor and lifeguard at the local sports complex, but now, with her best years behind her, the level of fitness required, together with advancing age, had led to the inevitable, and she had been gradually moved over to her present position in general admin.

With vanishingly little social contact outside work, she had put a brave face on it and wanted to stay beyond retirement, but the answer had been 'no'. Now she faced an uncertain future with little to look forward to.

In the meantime, as always, she tried to carry out her ragbag of a job description to the best of her ability, including her role as lost property officer. Previously it had been a somewhat random affair, but Jean made it her business to organise things properly, turning an unused box room into a lost property office. Unlike most of her other functions, it was a role which provided both interest and amusement, and Jean never failed to be amazed at how rarely owners returned to claim what might sometimes be quite high value items. At the other end of the scale, who would ask for the return of their knickers or underpants? So some items were soon binned while, after three weeks or maybe a month, the remainder went to the local charity shop.

Footwear of one sort or another was a relatively common occurrence but, on this morning, one example stood out from the little jumble of items left for her by the cleaners from the night before. While not especially familiar with men's shoes, the brown brogues attracted her attention immediately and, while speculating on how someone might have come to leave their outdoor shoes behind, she conducted a closer examination. They were clean, indeed polished, and worn but not excessively so, retaining some of their original elegance. On impulse, she raised one shoe to her nose and sniffed. Other than shoe polish and fine leather, nothing. No sweaty feet here then. A final inspection revealed the shoes to be size eight made by Churchs. Her dad, a local government administrator for many years, had always worn a suit. Nothing special, M & S at best, but he had always invested in really good shoes, and his shoemaker of choice had been Churchs. Coincidentally, he had also taken a size eight.

So, the brown brogues took their place on the shelf and, contrary to Jean's expectations, there they remained to give her a little warm feeling each morning, but also ongoing surprise that they had not been collected. She surmised that it might be one of the elders fitness group which met once a week in the gym but, having little to do with that side of things anymore, she could only ask among the instructors. Her enquiries provoked little interest and no information other than the fact that, on one occasion recently, the showers had been out of order and some of the elders would probably have gone home in their gym kit. Before long, the self-imposed deadline for moving uncollected items on, had arrived. A stickler for rules, even those of her own making, Jean wrestled with herself for a further week before the shoes joined the other items in the bag bound for Barnardo's.

If it was possible to miss a pair of shoes, owner unknown, then she did, noting the unfilled space on the shelf as she arrived the next morning. After fetching a coffee from the machine, she had just settled down at her desk when there was a knock at the door. In her best shouty voice, she commanded the visitor to enter but at first nothing happened. Everything was a squeeze in her tiny office, so it was a relief to see the door begin to open as she rose from her desk.

Suddenly, she found herself looking into a pair of enquiring brown eyes. The owner of the eyes looked to be a man in his mid-sixties, smartly dressed and well groomed. There was a hint of a decent aftershave. His voice was soft and educated with a flavour of Yorkshire. "Good morning. I realise it has been some time, but I wonder if a pair of shoes has been handed in."

Jean caught her breath but remained in control. "What sort of shoes?"

"Brown brogues. Do you know the sort I mean?"

"Yes, I think I do," said Jean, still keeping the lid on her growing anxiety. Well, it was not her responsibility, was it, if people chose to leave it so long?

"Only I've been really ill with the virus."

At this Jean leapt from her seat. "If you will go and sit in reception, I might, I say just might, be able to get them back for you." With that she grabbed her coat, ushered Brown-eyes out of her box room and set off at a trot.

Just around the corner, Barnardo's was not busy and, as she approached the counter, Jean could see that the volunteers were engaged in sorting out the donations from the day before. Alice, the long-time manager, looked up.

"Oh, hello Jean. Are you alright? You look a bit flustered."

"Yes, yes, I'm fine. It's just that I've been running."

"Running? You don't look dressed for it."

"No, no, not that sort of running, I just wanted to get round here as quickly as I could. Have you still got the stuff I brought in yesterday?"

"I'm not sure. I think it has all gone out on the shelves and Billy's in as usual, mooching about looking for stuff he can sell on at a profit. And now you're going to tell me that someone has come back for their stuff."

"Got it in one."

"So what are we looking for?"

"A pair of men's shoes, brown brogues." Alice came from behind the counter and together the two women went to the shoe rack: there they were.

Then came a voice from behind, "Can I come past?"

Alice pounced on the shoes cradling them in her arms.

"Oy! I was just comin' for these."

Alice turned, peering into the scruffy countenance that was nearly on her shoulder. "Well, Billy my lad, you're too late. These are spoken for."

At a more sedate pace, Jean made her way back to the leisure centre to find brown-eyes patiently waiting in reception. "I think these are yours."

"They are, they are. Thank you so much. I am so grateful. Where were they?"

"After a certain amount of time, we take unclaimed items to the charity shop. They were on the shelf in Barnardo's."

"And you saved them. I must repay you in some way; did you have to buy them back?"

"No, nothing like that. We have a very good relationship. They are very understanding."

"Well then I'll go round and make a donation."

"Just as you like." With that Jean made to return to her box room.

"Please, wait. I don't even know to whom I am indebted."

"You are not indebted to anyone. It's all part of the service, but if you must know, I'm Jean."

"Well, Jean. Thank you again most sincerely. I'm Jim, by the way."

Later that afternoon, Jean was still savouring one of the more interesting days at the Lost Property Office when there was a knock on the door. This time, she opened it to find Jim gazing at her over a large and stunningly beautiful bouquet of flowers.

"After this morning, I felt I just had to get you these."

Taken completely off-guard, Jean felt herself welling up a little.

"Sorry, sorry," Jim said. "I didn't mean to upset you."

"You haven't, it's fine really, it's just that… well thank you. You shouldn't have. They are beautiful."

"I hope your other half won't mind a man buying you flowers."

"Oh, it's nothing like that. There is no other half."

"Well, that's alright then. Oh no sorry I didn't mean … that came out wrong."

"It's alright. I've been on my own a long time. I'm used to it."

"Look, this might seem terribly forward, but most evenings I call in at The Royal just down the way for a bite to eat. I'm not much of a cook and I have never got used to eating on my own. I don't suppose you would care to join me."

Now completely flummoxed, Jean stammered, "Oh I don't know. I've not been in a pub for years, and anyway I'm not dressed."

"Well, you look absolutely fine to me. Besides, it's always quiet in the early evening. What time do you finish?"

"Five thirtyish."

"Shall I meet you down there or…"

"Oh, I don't know. I don't think I can walk into a pub on my own."

"Well then, I'll come here. Only I don't want to cause you any embarrassment."

"There's not much chance of that. The receptionist is a temp, and if I disappeared tomorrow, I think it would be days before anyone noticed."

Back in her box room, she felt stunned and in a state of disbelief. Was she really going to the pub in an hour's time with a complete stranger? But already, he did not feel like a stranger. Indeed, that odd feeling of familiarity on first sight was still with her, and remained with her as they walked down to the pub together.

Even now she wonders how they managed to eat, for they talked, oh how they talked, and by the end she had learned that his wife had succumbed to cancer four years earlier and, despite her plea that he should not be lonely on her account, he had struggled. Only in this last year had he begun to emerge from the shadow of Martha's death.

"If these last years have taught me anything, it is that life is short and putting your hopes and dreams on hold leads nowhere."

And by the end of that same meal, Jim had learned that Jean had married young and had been blissfully happy in that first year before the war. Stan was a member of the Territorial Army Reserve and had received his call up papers earlier than most. On a sunny day in June, they had kissed and embraced on a windy railway station platform, and she never saw him again. 'Missing in Action',

Year on year, she never gave up hope. The idea that, any day, Stan might walk through the door and find another man with his feet under his table, sitting on his chair, was intolerable to her and remained in the background as an insurmountable obstacle to any new relationship. In the end, she had stopped trying and then, almost without realising, had ceased to dwell on the past. But by then, being alone had become a habit. Looking back now, it all seemed a million miles away and more like a bad dream from which she might just be about to emerge.

Two years on, sitting before her dressing table mirror, she can see, reflected in the glass, Jim sitting up in bed engrossed in his novel, the novel he will immediately set aside when she slips in beside him. Shifting her gaze back to her own image, she sees that person who, for so long had been a stranger, lost in her own land and now, found, a stranger no more.

A Very Serious Conversation

Bob Mynors

A white Volvo coupé hurtled along the street, tyres squealing as it took the corner too quickly. It screamed to a halt outside a smart apartment building. From the car, a tall, dark-haired man emerged, slim, stylish, handsome. He bounded up the steps. At the door, he punched a code into the keypad and the door swung open. He entered: there was someone inside with whom he needed a serious conversation, and he was in no mood to wait

He took the stairs to the second floor rather than wait for the lift. He heard the concierge ring through to announce him. At the apartment door, he rang the bell and the door opened smoothly

Inside the apartment, he walked along a corridor that opened into a - *what might it be called*? *A drawing room*? He saw her sitting in a red leather armchair at the far side of the room. She smiled. She was younger than he was. She was also most attractive, and her smile was infectious. He found he had no choice but to smile back. "I imagine there is no need for me to introduce myself," he said

"None at all," she replied. "I recognised you the moment I saw you at the party,"

He took a pack of cigarettes from his pocket. She accepted one when it was offered. He lit it for her. She drew on the cigarette and blew out a cloud of smoke which formed into a ring that floated upwards, coming to rest briefly above his head. Having witnessed reactions to this unlikely phenomenon on many occasions in the past, he allowed a hint of his own smile to form at one side of his mouth and he raised an eyebrow slightly, but his gaze remained intently on her

"You're the famous Simon Templar," she purred. "You're the Saint."

"You're a clever girl. But I feel you owe me an explanation." Her smile broadened into an equally attractive grin. He continued. "You have been prying into my background with rather more persistence than makes me comfortable, Lady Teresa."

Settling back, she said, "I see you also know who I am. Would that not count as prying too?" She threw back her dark, shining hair provocatively and looked askance at the Saint

He replied, "If I weren't concerned that it would make me sound like some kind of a petulant eight-year-old, I might say you started it. But I think it would be more productive if I invited you to explain why you have been making such detailed enquiries about me. What possible interest can the Lady Teresa Fitzrussell have in the humble Simon Templar?"

"Oh, do come off it, darling." Tilting her head slightly, she added in an aside, "I may call you darling, may I not?"

He nodded

"Well, darling – the reason I made my enquiries … No – if I told you, you'd think I was being silly."

"I'm sure no-one would ever consider you silly."

"Well – you remember we met originally at that do in April - Abigail Trentham's birthday, though I'm sure she's too old to have any more birthdays now."

"I remember, though no-one had the grace to introduce us. It was at Fitz's in Russell Square." After the briefest pause, he asked, "You're not related, are you?"

Giggling, she told him, "Of course not. Though it can be fun sometimes to tease people and let them think I am."

"It was the party with that noisy pop group playing in the corner, wasn't it?"

"Noisy pop group?" Lady Teresa sounded almost offended. "That was McFly. They were big once, and Abi always had the hots for their drummer, so it was easy for her to get them to come and play. And I think that the hots she had for Harry, he's the drummer, used to get pretty steamy back in the day, but he's married now, to a violinist or something. In fact, I think the party raised money for a charity Harry's wife supports – brain injuries or something."

The Saint was beginning to feel that Lady Teresa was being deliberately evasive, so he said, "That is all very laudable, I'm sure, but it hardly answers my question. Why have you been prying into my past? My back story as you might call it?"

"I'm sorry, darling." She giggled again. "I do allow myself to get side-tracked. But please – you're standing. Do pull up a chair." Whilst the Saint did so, Lady Teresa finally began her story. "It was shortly after Abi's party. I went to visit my grandmamma. She is a wonderful old lady and she so likes to hear about all the things I get up to – well, most of them. I don't tell her everything, obviously."

Making eye-contact, he simply said, "Obviously."

She continued. "Naturally I told her about the party. She's known the Trenthams all her life, so she was jolly interested. And of course I mentioned meeting a devilishly handsome man called Simon Templar."

"I am flattered."

"Well don't be. Granny is 102 years old and she gets terribly confused sometimes. She obviously had you confused with someone she knew when she was young and that was ages ago, before the war. She married my grandpa in the 1930s. He was the 4th Earl. She must have known this man, the one she's confused you with, before that. But when I showed her a picture of you on my phone, she said, 'Yes. That's him. Simon Templar, the Saint. Oh, he was a heartbreaker. Everyone who knew him wanted him, but he soared above us all.' That was the point at which I poured her another small glass of gin and dismissed what she had said. But in the following days, I found I couldn't dismiss it entirely from my mind, so I decided to find out for myself which of your ancestors she could have been talking about."

Again, the Saint's smile curled and his eyebrow lifted. "I'm flattered again – that you have a photograph of me on your phone."

"Don't flatter yourself, Mr Templar." For the first time, an edge of annoyance crept into Lady Teresa's voice. "I have a photograph of Abi's party on my phone – several of them, in fact. You just happen to be in a couple of them

"But, back at the real point of this conversation, I've searched everywhere I can and have not managed to find out a single thing about your background – just the society stuff. And that's pretty unusual in the modern world. We're forever being told that our personal data is being held on servers all over the place, even on servers up in space, but not Simon Templar – oh no. I can find out all kinds of things about your exploits, but I have failed completely to find out anything at all about who you are or where you come from. So that's why you are here, Simon Templar, so that I can find out who you actually are, what your origins are, and why my poor confused grandmamma thinks you're the man she was in love with in about

1930 or something. So – what do you have to say for yourself?"

He drew himself up in his chair, took a breath, and began to speak. "There is a very simple explanation, Lady Teresa, and I hope you won't mind me saying so, but you will be disappointed not to have worked it out for yourself. I am, you see, a fictional character …"

She gasped slightly

"… and fictional characters don't age, not in the same way that real people do, especially if they are characters of a certain type, and especially not in the eyes of the more casual observer. It's for the same reason that I can drive a car that's been out of production for decades and for which spare parts long ago ceased to be available. Yet it never lets me down. It starts first time every time and has never seen an inspection ramp or an MoT testing station."

Lady Teresa broke in at this point. "What are you talking about, fictional character? This is the real world. You are real. I am real. This chair is real." She slapped the leather arm of the chair and the noise it made sounded real enough

"Are you sure? Might it not simply be that we are well-written, well-described by our author? I am just the kind of fictional character people can really believe in."

Lady Teresa was far too disciplined to allow her own jaw to drop, though many others would not now have had such strength of mind

The Saint continued. "You're an educated woman. You read literary criticism. You are aware that the ability to evoke an air of realism in their work – verisimilitude some call it – is a highly-prized quality amongst writers. And in this world of fiction, some characters are privileged never to suffer the ravages of age. It all depends on whether we have the legs for it."

Blushing was something Lady Teresa was no longer used to, but she blushed now and pulled at the hem of her short skirt, yet failed to cover more of her thigh than was exposed

"I'm not talking about physical legs, darling. I may call you darling?" Again she pulled at her hem. "I'm talking about literary legs, character legs. I'm talking about having series potential rather than being simply a walk-on sort of character."

"Are you trying to tell me that you're not the only fictional one in this conversation? That I'm fictional too? That I don't really exist?"

"I'm afraid that must be the case. You exist all right, but you must be fictional because you are in my story. But look on the bright side. There may be people reading us all over the world – thousands of people, millions of people, and in many different languages. We may be in a classic that will be read repeatedly for decades to come, for centuries."

Lady Teresa was far from happy at this. "Or we may be in a scribbled piece hurriedly cobbled together by some wannabe in a writers group in a god-forsaken northern city, only ever to be read by a dozen or so saddos with nothing better to do with their time." Her voice trembled. She seemed on the verge of tears

"It might be worse even than that, darling. We may have been scribbled in the back of a teenage girl's notebook never to be seen by anyone."

This was too much for Lady Teresa Fitzrussell. She stood, ran to the edge of the page and dived into the void outside the narrative. At this, Simon Templar felt uneasy, very uneasy. The feeling was strongest in the pit of his stomach and in the soles of his feet. He felt faint. He tried to stand but hadn't the strength in his body. He knew what was happening. His narrative thread was unravelling. He was losing his literary legs and would soon lose everything else. He would appear no more. Never had any of his many followers – followers of the books, the radio episodes, the TV series, the films - seen or even suspected such a look of shock on the face of the famous Simon Templar. Never had anyone seen or even imagined this Startled Saint

The group theme that inspired this story was 'pub names'. The Startled Saint was a pub in West Malling, Kent, but it is no more

Shades of Lapis Blue

Graham Bloodworth

"Hi Olive, it's only me."

She walked down the hall with a bag of shopping, knowing her client would be in the front room.

"Want a cuppa?"

"If you're making one, dear."

She filled the kettle and, while waiting for it to boil, put away the groceries. It never ceased to amaze her the things you found in cupboards, mainly out of date. Yet they provided a touchstone for that generation, condensed milk, Fray Bentos pies, although she shuddered at a box of powdered egg that should be in a museum along with an ancient tin of Spam.

She went about the routine of making the tea, warming the pot because Olive hated tea bags. Once this was completed, she added to the tray cups, saucers, teaspoons, milk jug, tea strainer, a bowl of sugar cubes and a plate of bourbon biscuits, then carried it into the living room.

This was Olive's little empire, where she held court, so to speak. The best room was off limits, only opened for a select group. Although there were precious few of those nowadays. She had often wondered what was so special about this one room.

The tea ceremony played out, with biscuits offered and conversation about this and that. This was difficult because Olive sometimes lost the plot, talking to her long-deceased mother. She made sure that Olive had taken her medication and was comfortable. There was never enough time on these calls: the agency allowed only so much time with each client. Overrun with one and she had to make it up by cutting short another client or put in unpaid overtime.

Olive had nodded off.

Oh well, that made her life easier. But on walking down the hallway, she stopped at the best room door. A blue light was shining through the gap at the bottom of the door. More importantly, the key was in the lock. Surely it would not hurt just to look in. Just as she reached for the key, the light went out. Now that was strange. Turning the key, then the brass doorknob, she pushed the door open, almost expecting it to scream out like in the horror movies. Yet it swung on well-oiled hinges, revealing a darkened void. The heavy velvet curtains resisted the outside light; but her hand found the light switch.

The room was a riot of china collectables. She knew of Royal Doulton and Poole pottery, from watching antiques programmes on the television.

Yet what caught her eye was a whole table full of Beswick horses, mares, colts, fillies. Even stables, hedges and ceramic water troughs, a fortune in this one room. Walking over, she took a closer look. A figure of a male groom caught her eye, and she picked it up to marvel at the detail, next a ploughman behind a pair of Shire draughts, plough tilling the soil. On a pony taking a jump over a fence, close up she could see the look of apprehension: this must be the girl's first big obstacle. Then an exquisite thoroughbred mare. Would Olive miss just one piece?

Now where did that thought come from? Theft was not worth costing her the job. Movement across the other side of the table drew her curiosity because the figure was not on a base, but rearing on its back legs. Moreover, it was a beautiful Lapis blue with a white forelock. How could it balance like that?

Needing no further encouragement, she took a few steps to where her hand hovered over it. Yet, as she lowered her hand to pick it up, it swung around and bit her.

"Ouch!"

Scarlet drops formed. The room spun. The equine's eyes flashed.

Words formed in her head.

"You are not the first." A pause. *"A stallion protects the herd."*

A golden glow formed around her; and she placed a hand on the table to stop herself falling. The hand stuck, morphing into a hoof. The rest of her shrank and began the strange journey of disappearing down the armhole of her uniform, leaving her clothes lying on the floor. The rest of her had now been transformed into a mare in miniature, the china surface hardening, but not before a scream that became a whinny of terror. The door closed slowly; and the light went out.

Olive woke and shuffled to the best room. The key turned in the lock, the door swung open and the light came on, unbidden. Her younger self walked over to the table, pleased that mother had bought another mare for her to play with.

The Wedding Do

P Wright

Knocking on the door of my parents' home and walking straight in, I shouted "It's only me - Helen."

"Oh, we weren't expecting you tonight. Are you on your own?" Carol, my mother, asked.

"Yes. Phil has gone to football. I just wanted to come round and give you the news first," I said smiling. My father lowered his newspaper with interest.

"Oh, how wonderful we're going to be grandparents!" my mother exclaimed.

My father looked at me, I could see the delight on his face.

"No Mom, that's not it," I told her. I never realised they would think that.

Mom looked puzzled. "Well what else could it be?" she asked, disappointed.

"We have decided to get married. Just a small private affair. We've lived together for five years now, so we think it's the right time," I told them. My father went back to reading his paper.

"Oh, George, that's wonderful news, isn't it?" she said with less enthusiasm than at the thought of being grandparents. "You'll need a new suit, of course, George. A June wedding will be lovely. You'll have to have the banns read at St Mary's, of course. How many bridesmaids are you having? Of course, Cousin Jane, she's very photogenic."

"Mom, please stop! We just want a quiet register office wedding with Phil's parents, you and Dad and a couple of friends. A more intimate affair."

"Quite right too," Dad chimed in.

"Of course, darling, but haven't you always dreamed of a beautiful church wedding, with bridesmaids and flowers and what about the reception?"

"Mom, we have lived together for the past five years. I don't think it would be appropriate. And all that expense!"

"Ridiculous, spending all that money on one day," Dad said, listening behind his newspaper.

"George, shut up. Haven't you always said it would be the highlight of your life walking your daughter down the aisle?"

"Have I? I don't remember," he replied.

"Of course you have, George. It's what every father wants to do!" Mom shouted towards the newspaper.

I could sense my mother's brain ticking. "Just a quiet informal wedding, Mom."

"A quiet do, but in a church, please darling," she uttered, with a crestfallen face."

"I don't think Phil will agree to that …." I didn't get chance to finish the sentence.

"A register office is so cold and I'm sure you will regret it in years to come. Everyone will think you've *got* to get married," she said smiling.

Dad lowered his newspaper. "Leave the girl alone, Carol. It's her big day."

"Exactly George, a big day. I know you're only thinking about the cost!"

"Mom, it just doesn't feel right getting married in a church."

"Rubbish. Charlene down the road got married in the church and she was seven months pregnant," she said, miming a big belly. "You don't have to be religious nowadays to get married in a church. Your father would be so honoured and happy to give you away. Wouldn't you, George?"

"Whatever you say, dear," he replied, speaking through the newspaper. He knew it was no good arguing with his wife. She always had the last word.

"I'll be off now, Mom. See you later." I hugged her and kissed Dad on the top of his head, his bald spot.

"Just think about what I've said. I'm sure Phil will agree with me. I'll ring you later. Bye darling." Mom gave a little wave and a big smile as I left.

"What time's tea, Carol?" George asked.

"Oh, you can get fish and chips later. I've such a lot to do and organise," Carol replied as she picked up the phone. "Hi Jane. It's Carol. I've got some great news. Our Helen and Phil are getting married. She just wants a quiet do, you know, just the family and a few friends. Yes, of course that will include your Becky and Trevor and their children, maybe little Olivia could be a bridesmaid. I'll ask our Helen. No, you're the first to know. I'll ring our Rob now. Bye love."

"Shall I go to the chippy now?" George asked.

"Not yet, George. I've just to ring our Rob, then Pat and Joe."

Two hours later George asked again. "Should I go to the chippy now? I think they close at ten thirty tonight."

"Oh George, that's all you think about - your belly. Yes, go now and only get small portions. We don't want to go to bed on a heavy stomach. We'll have to watch our weight as well; we don't want to look massive on the wedding photos, do we?"

"What are you doing anyway?" he asked.

"The wedding list, of course!" she replied.

"But you heard what Helen said, 'a small intimate do, no fuss'."

"Oh George. Just go for the supper. I'm sure Helen is only thinking about the expense!" Carol replied, irritated, still writing.

"Tea, you mean. She's not the only one worried about the expense," he whispered.

◇

I arrived home and prepared our evening meal. Phil would be back home anytime now.

"Hi love. Tea won't be long. Was it a good game?" I asked. I could tell it wasn't by looking at the false smile.

"Not bad, the pitch was waterlogged. It should have been cancelled actually," he replied, leaving his sports bag in the hall, then going into the living room and picking up the remote. "How long will tea be? Did you tell your mom about us getting married?" he shouted.

After tea, Phil loaded the dishwasher while I loaded the washer with the contents of his sports bag. Then we both flopped down on the sofa.

"Mom and Dad were pleased about the wedding, but I think they would have been more pleased if I'd told them I was pregnant." I told him. "Mom would like us to have a church wedding."

"I thought we agreed, a quick ceremony, a meal then off on honeymoon," Phil said, taking hold of my hand.

"I totally agree. I just hope Mom will understand."

46

◊

Carol couldn't sleep, "Do you want a drink bringing up, George?" she asked, waking him up.

"What? What's the matter, are you OK?"

"I'm going downstairs for a mug of Horlicks. Do you want one bringing up?"

"No love. Can't you sleep?"

"We've got a lot to think about. A wedding doesn't organise itself, you know. I think I'll start a list while I'm having my drink. You go back to sleep." Then Carol asked a sleepy George, "Do you think your Uncle Patrick and Aunt Martha will come over from Ireland for the wedding?"

George rolled over and pretended to be asleep.

Drinking her Horlicks, Carol put pen to paper and started the list:

1. See the vicar
2. Venue for Reception
3. Brides Dress
4. Mother of the Brides outfit
5. A new suit for George
6. Invitations
7. Guest list

8. Caterers
9. Band
10. Flowers

And the list went on and on and on. Eventually though, she went back to bed and put the list on her bedside table, just in case she woke up and thought of something else.

Next day, Carol started writing the guest list. Should she ask Helen about the bridesmaids and who would be maid of honour? Maybe she would consult Helen first. George agreed that would be a good idea.

Carol had already filled one page of the guest list with family members, and decided now to start on friends and neighbours.

◊

The following Saturday, I went over to my parents to ask if Mom wanted anything fetching in from the shops in town.

"I thought I could go with you today; I'll just get my bag. See you later George,' she shouted to Dad who was watching football and never answered.

Strange, I thought, Mom never wants to go into town. Getting in the car, I asked her, "Do you want anything in particular, Mom?"

"I thought I would have a look around for an outfit for the wedding. Maybe you could look for a dress at the same time."

"Mom, I've already got a dress, the one I wore to Ascot, remember?"

"Not that flowered one with the pink bolero?" she said, screwing up her nose.

"Yes, that one. I've only worn it once and I love it," I replied, a little annoyed. "You said it looked lovely and would look nice for a wedding."

"Well, yes it did look nice, but for a wedding guest, not the bride."

"I've told you, Mom, we don't want a fuss, just the register office, a meal and then we're off on our honeymoon," I said as firmly as I could. "Anyway, it's your wedding anniversary soon. Why don't you plan something for you and Dad? Go away somewhere nice and exotic."

"You know your dad doesn't like flying. He's a home bird. Cornwall is the farthest he'll travel."

Trying to keep off the subject of my wedding, I went on, "What about a party then? Something to mark the occasion?"

"I'll think about it. Now let's see what Jacque Verts has for the mother of the bride." The assistant came straight over as Mom lifted a dress off the rail.

"That will be a lot of expense for a couple of hours, don't you think?" I told her.

"Not for my only daughter's wedding, and I think you would look beautiful in a long white satin dress. Your father would love to walk you down the aisle in a lovely gown, and Phil's face would be a picture seeing you in it."

"No, Mom, it's not what we want. No fuss, remember?" I told her, agitated.

"It wouldn't be any fuss. I would love to arrange everything; you wouldn't have anything to do. I love that dress in the window. What do you think, Helen?" Mom asked.

"Well, it's pink flowered, a bit like mine, don't you think?" I told her. "Why don't you go for a nice blue, or that petty lilac one?"

"No, I think I will try the pink one. It has a lovely matching hat," she replied as she went into the fitting room.

I looked at the price tag. It was ridiculous. But when she came out of the fitting room, I had to admit it looked beautiful, and a perfect fit too. I felt she had bought it deliberately, so I would have to buy a new dress. Then I thought it was me that was being unreasonable. Of course, she wanted to look nice, and I told her so.

"Now I've got my dress, shall we have a look for one for you?"

"Well, we both can't wear pink now, can we?" I told her as she steered me into the department store.

"I'll just have a look at the court shoes in here," she said. "Why don't you go and have a look in the bridal section, and I'll come over to you when I've bought some shoes and matching bag?"

I knew it was no good arguing with Mom and I didn't want to stand around while she was trying on shoes. As I wandered over to the bridal section, I saw a beautiful tropical print, halter neck dress. I tried it on. I loved it. I bought it - perfect for our honeymoon. Then I sauntered over to the bridal section, not interested. Could there be something wrong with me, I thought, not wanting one of these masterpieces? And so expensive, the less there was of them the more money they were. A sales lady came over. "This one would suit you dear. It is very similar to the one Kate wore at her wedding. Or perhaps something more flamboyant like this one."

She held up a large meringue dress in front of me, just as Mom came dashing over. "Oh Helen, that's beautiful. Have you tried it on?"

"No, Mom, it's not quite me. I don't really want a big dress or a big fuss." I turned and looked at the disappointed sales assistant. "Sorry." She hung the dress back on the rail as I walked away.

Mom hurried after me. "Helen, what's the matter with you? It wouldn't have hurt just to try it on."

"No, Mom I won't be railroaded into anything I don't want," I told her firmly. "I'll order something online. I'm not paying anything like you've just paid for a couple of hours at the most."

"Your Dad is paying. You don't want the bridesmaids looking better than the bride surely."

"For the last time Mom, no bridesmaids, no fuss."

Mom sat silent all the way back home. "Aren't you coming in for a cuppa?" Mom asked softly.

"No thank you, I have to get home. We're out with Karen and Tom tonight," I said kissing Mom on the cheek. Then I drove home, letting out a big sigh.

52

That evening, we met up with Karen and Tom. I explained to them the fuss Mom was making and explained that I think she was trying to make up for the wedding she wanted but couldn't afford at the time. I explained to Phil it was making me very anxious.

"Listen. I think I may have a solution," Karen said, "although it may not make everyone happy." We put our heads together. It was a great plan *if* we could pull it off.

Phil and I called in to see Mom the next day. "Phil and I have been discussing a few things and think the last Saturday in June would be a good date, is that OK with you, Mom. We have an appointment with the vicar at St Mary's next week."

"Oh, that's wonderful, isn't it, George?" Mom's face lit up. "We'll get you a suit from M&S next week. A nice light grey. Oh, is yours that colour Phil, or do you want all the men dressed the same?"

"No Carol, whatever George wants is fine. You know, low key, no fuss."

"I'm so glad you have changed your mind; I would have loved a church wedding."

Phil looked to me, and we smiled at each other.

53

The following week, I rang Mom. "I hope you can help, Mom. We have a problem reading the banns. We both have to work late for the next few weeks, and we wondered if you and Dad could go for us. Reverend Thomas said it would be fine in the circumstances." I asked pleadingly.

"No problem is it, George? What about the guest list and reception? I was wondering Channing Hotel."

"Mom, whatever you think. I'm afraid we're both so busy with work. If you could write out our side of the family for guests, I will do Phil's side of the family. If you have time, of course."

"No worries, darling. Leave it all to me."

"Thanks Mom, you're a treasure. What would I do without you and Dad? Love you both."

"It's our pleasure, darling, well mine your dad's never been any good at organising anything."

"I heard that. My plastic card's doing the work for me," Dad shouted.

I shouted back, "Thanks Dad. I'm sure it will be worth it to keep Mom happy."

◊

Our next conversation was a few days later when Mom rang me to let me know the hotel reception was all arranged and ask if she should let me have the menus. I told her I trusted her judgement - whatever she thought best. Then she said she had sent out the invitations and asked had I done the same for Phil's family. I told her actually there would only be Phil's parents attending as his brother and wife were on holiday, and he wasn't that close to the rest of his family. Mom said she had booked the photographer and I told her our friend Tom was going to video the day.

After further conversations about flowers, band or disco, champagne or prosecco, and of course Aunty Betty doing the cake, I had nothing to do but plan the honeymoon. Great.

The last Saturday in June arrived. We had told Mom and Dad we would see them at the church. Mom couldn't understand. "It's tradition. You're asking for bad luck." But nevertheless, there was nothing she could do about it.

Our good friends Tom and Karen were waiting on the church steps as everyone arrived. It started raining, Tom ushered everyone inside as quickly as he could.

Tom stood by the vicar's side Karen stood with the video camera recording everything, with the permission of the vicar, of course. Tom turned on the large screen at the side of the altar. Everyone looked confused, especially Mom.

The screen burst into life. Phil appeared on the screen grinning in his shorts and tee shirt and me in my tropical print, halter neck dress, turquoise sea and pure white sands with palm trees in the background.

"Hi Mom, Dad. Sorry to have had to do this, but you know I don't like a fuss. But I want you to enjoy your special day. Happy anniversary. I hope Phil and I are as happy as you and Dad have been all these years."

I held up my left hand and waved it in front of the screen showing my wedding ring. Phil waved at the screen "Hi Mom and Dad, have a good day. See you all when we get home in a couple of weeks. It's so hot here. Just going for a dip. Bye."

I shouted, "Mom, stop crying and enjoy your day. We'll see you when we get home. Love you both, bye."

Phil and I shouted, "Bye everyone. Have a great time. Thank you all for coming." We could see them all waving back to us: technology is a wonderful thing!

◇

Tom turned off the computer and screen. The vicar took his place at the altar.

"So, ladies and gentlemen, as you may have guessed, this is not a wedding ceremony but a renewal of vows. Would Carol and George like to come to the altar, please?"

Carol stared at the vicar, tears rolling down her cheeks, her hand over her open mouth, not knowing what to do and, for once, lost for words. George took Carol's hand and squeezed it tight as they made their way forward to renew their vows. Everyone clapped and cheered. The rest of the day went exactly as Carol had planned it. The first dance was theirs. George held her tight as they waltzed around, whispering that, after all these years, he still loved her, and she kissed him gently on the lips.

"I just wish Helen and Phil were here," she told Tom.

Tom leaned over to Carol. "Don't worry. They'll see it all when they get back from the Caribbean.

We'll all watch the video together, and I'll make you your own special copy."

That night in the honeymoon suite of the hotel, George said, "So, Carol, what a day, eh?" as they got into bed.

"Oh, George. It's been the highlight of my life. What a wonderful daughter we have. I can't wait until they get home to tell them all about it."

A year later, whilst I was visiting my parents as usual, I said, "Mom, I have some news to tell you."

"Oh no," she replied. Dad put down his newspaper with a worried look on his face. That wasn't the reply I was expecting. Mom ran over and flung her arms around me. "A baby that's wonderful news!"

"Yes it is, Grandma and Grandad."

Ghost Haiku

Diane Bingham

The lecture hall was full, packed with students eager to listen to the renowned and erudite speaker whose topic of the day was "The Art of Haiku". The professor strode towards the platform and acknowledged the applause with a casual wave of his hand.

As the sound subsided, a young man, crammed onto the back row, searched for sight of her. And there she was, centre stage front row, looking as serious as always, concentrating and hanging on every word. She was so studious, so scholarly, and he adored her. But would she ever notice him?

The lecture finished to further rapturous applause and the professor announced the names of those selected for the tutorial group. The young man held his breath. He dared to hope. And he was rewarded.

The tutorial room was the professor's study, small and intimate. The relaxed nature of the surroundings masked the anxiety of the students. Six of the seven smiled nervously, each pleased to be one of the chosen few. But she was sombre, her dark eyes flashed. She portrayed the gravity of the situation. They were to be judged.

The professor leaned back in his armchair, hands behind his head, controlling the space as he posed the questions. "As I said in the lecture, haikus focus on a brief moment in time, juxtaposing two images and creating a sudden sense of enlightenment. Can you see any inbuilt contradiction in this?" He looked to her for an answer.

Calmly she replied that if there are two lines about something beautiful in nature, and then a third line that is a complete surprise, this second image so often breaks the spell and leads to incongruence, whereas Basho had talked of glimmers of hope in small simple things revealing connectedness. "This", she said, "could be seen as an innate contradiction of the form."

The professor looked delighted with his star pupil and turned to the young man. "And why do you suppose that enjambment is not encouraged in haiku?"

The young man hesitated; a rabbit caught in the spotlight. Then, self-consciously and after a false start he replied. "Rhythm is an essential characteristic of haiku and pauses between the lines enhance the poem, particularly when read aloud. Where two lines of a haiku are enjambed, there is the risk that one line will run into the other, eliminating any pause between those lines. Enjambment makes it more difficult to enjoy the rhythm." He stuttered to a close and looked down at his shoes before glancing upwards and towards her.

Solemn eyes sought his
Across her earnest face came
The ghost of a smile

Cake and Coronet

Sue Allott

The stage was set. We all gathered, the committee and I, for the Coronation celebrations. My husband and I were to be the king and queen, and be on stage for the 3.00 pm cream tea opening. Suitably gowned and coroneted, we strutted around the community hall dressed to the nines, mingling with the courtiers and commoners. Everyone was enjoying themselves with much laughter.

Local farmer Bob Munroe was to give 'the speech' and was trying hard to keep his farm dogs, and a 'suspicious corgi', all dressed suitably with bow ties and ribbons, on their leads.

The whole village, with great excitement, had come together for this occasion. Soldiers of the guard were milling around dressed in their red tunics, swords at their sides – just in case an incident occurred.

The band began to play, the Lord Mayor approached the microphone on stage, adjusting his beautiful chain of office. This chain had nearly disappeared a few times into the realms of local crime, but fortunately it had never left the premises of the mayoral parlour, such was the security, we were proud to say, at the times of the incidents.

The local constabulary were circulating the garden perimeter, just in case they might have an exciting day apprehending someone.

The mayor announced the maypole dancing was about to begin, and asked everyone, please, to support the children during this event.

Afterwards, the dog show was on the programme. Needless to say, Bob's suspicious Corgi won paws down and strutted around the garden with a huge blue rosette attached to his body harness.

The sun shone and a light breeze drifted through the surrounding trees, gently lifting the edges of many ribbon-adorned sun hats.

Life indeed was very enjoyable. Children were laughing, adults chattering and drinking their chosen sups. The food was wonderful. Sandwiches had been so neatly made and cut into those tiny triangles, amidst the jokes of 'more tea, vicar?', 'one lump or two?' and 'cucumber sandwich, anyone?' It was all good fun. I was proud of the way everything had turned out.

Then it came for the toast to the king and queen. We had just returned from the coconut shy where my husband, the King, had knocked down the biggest coconut, thereby winning the biggest teddy bear on the stand. Nearby, I was graciously whooping and smiling broadly. We then made our way to the stage, up the steps, waving and from there we would be cheered and applauded. A company of soldiers led the way, then stood behind us and at each end of the stage.

Suddenly, one of the soldiers, to my left, swiftly withdrew his sword from its sheath and, with one mighty swipe, flung it across the necks of my husband and I. Red was flowing, followed by rivers of white. Our heads rolled onto the floor and the whole place was in an uproar, people shouting towards the soldier, "Traitor! To the scaffold with him!"

A loud scream was heard, choking and coughing, it was then I realised these sounds were coming from my throat. It was actually me who was screaming. My mouth had fallen open and I was so dry. I'd fallen asleep on the settee after a very tiring day helping to set up the community hall for our Coronation event after the marquee had been put up. I found myself holding a fallen plate with the remains of a large piece of Victoria sponge cake.

My mouth, of course, was dribbling jam and cream, blobs of which had managed to fall onto the front of my white blouse. It began to occur to me that the figures in my dream, were in fact not my husband and I but replicas of the rice paper figures that stood on top of the central table display, a magnificent Victoria sponge cake, a large piece of which I'd secretly stolen during the afternoon, brought it home and as my eyes were bigger than my belly, had fallen asleep. Justice had been served because I shouldn't have been so wickedly greedy! I fell back onto the settee, groaning and feeling sick.

Sweat? I was bathed in it.

As If … If Only

Jacqueline Blackburn

'As if ... if only'. Those phrases - what do they mean? Not much you might say. Is it life at its most existential or life at its most conditional? More to the point, that's how it felt being on a gap year where I went nowhere and met no one. What some of the more pretentious students in my old A-level English Lit class would have called 'a liminal space' - one ripe with possibilities.

But that was when they were discussing *Othello* or something like Shelley's 'To a Skylark', not some would-be student stranded in the dead zone between school and uni like me. Anyway, it didn't feel like any sort of generative space to me, more like a ton weight on my chest. Even so, it seemed loads better than its more scratchy alternative, action; that felt too much like a road map with no directions.

The threat of the latter followed me round like a yappy terrier snapping at my heels on every one of those gap year days. It was usually accompanied by imperatives such as 'Just do it' if it was a so-called mate or 'Faint heart never won the fair lady' if it was my dad. What was that even meant to mean, I wondered? It was as opaque as it was chivalric and, clearly, anachronistic. A bit like dad really, hovering around in the background like a phantom presence, never fully there, just hinting that he might make his presence felt if it ever came to it.

Better than mum though. Her statements came bookended with a look that bored right through me. Every time she said it, she was 'doing something' like feverishly drying glasses, holding them up to the light to check for stains, or charging round the kitchen, car keys in hand, on her way to choir practice or one of the endless committee meetings she attended back then. You see mum just can't sit still. Never could and, I fear, never will. On the rare occasions when she's watching TV, she fiddles with the remote, constantly switching channels, her head bobbing up and down like a demented woodpecker to the sound of clacking knitting needles. And it wasn't as if dad or I ever got to wear any of the hats, scarves or gloves she churned out as she glanced at the screen a million times a second. That's because they weren't for us. Put simply, we just weren't needy enough. Put even more bluntly, neither of us was sliding around in a rat-infested trench nor did we attend food banks, and we weren't in receipt of universal credit. Come to think of it, neither was mum, so what was it all about?

Well, at the risk of sounding like someone who's just finished Freud's 'Interpretation of Dreams' (which I had)', I needed to find out as the year wore on and I got more and more worn down by mum's constant sniping. In time I became equally fascinated with what could be called mum's own 'failure to progress'. It was a familiar phrase since it was the reason the examiner gave me for failing my driving test on that day some six months before I was due to start uni at one of the plate glass institutions that mum thought so deplorable. It summed up everything I felt so succinctly; it felt uncanny, as though it was an essential part of my destiny or fate, as somebody like Euripides would have put it all those years ago. The trouble was it appealed to mum's sense that I lacked purpose like the perfectly sized coin that slides ever so neatly into its slot. There was never any chance of a strategic hug, a consolatory cup of tea or a glass of the wine that mum gulped down every evening at five on the dot when she heard about the instructor's deliberations. No, instead there was just a deep sigh and a glance heavenward as she marched towards the greenhouse, or orangery as she called it, when some of her smarter friends called round. She held the secateurs aloft, and the plants didn't stand a chance.

So, there I stood, that standard phrase 'failure to progress' so casually dropped by an examiner, itching to move on to the next hapless driver, who seemingly defined my entire existence, according to mum anyway. The evening before, mum had urged me to have an early night so I could focus more clearly on what she called 'the job in hand'. No more 'what ifs' or 'if onlys', just keep your 'eyes on the prize'; a new phrase that had crept into mum's vocabulary ever since she'd heard about a friend's daughter's successful start-up business selling cupcakes to other start-ups in the city's cultural quarter. Enquiries made by me about the longevity of her business plan, or just what she'd do when the money ran out, were met with icy derision by mum.

'She'll do what she's always done, think outside the box, use her noddle.'

This latter statement was accompanied by mum tapping the side of her head whilst sorting through a pile of junk mail on the dining room table. 'Unlike you,' she might as well have said, 'nobody said she wasn't a multi-tasker.'

With just six months to go before uni, I decided to take some action on my own behalf. Mum's comments were as tedious as they were predictable. I had to do something to break up her prickly monologues, so I decided to tackle her on her own failure to progress. In her case, it wasn't so much that she'd failed to progress, more like progress hadn't taken her where she wanted to go. Her penchant for dogmatic phrases, imperatives and non-sequiturs sat uneasily alongside sighs, silences and a growing tendency to 'zone out' in the middle of conversations. So, yeah, I'd prod her in some uncomfortable places just like the weeds she was busily yanking out in front of the greenhouse. It didn't take a genius to work out she'd got her own barren patch of ground to attend to if she was ever to progress.

'There's no time like the present' was another phrase that cropped up on a regular basis, so I decided to take her at her word. By that time, mum had chucked her trowel to one side and moved inside the greenhouse, which resembled our spare room full of cases and boxes that no one wanted but didn't feel ready to throw away. Seed trays and swaying columns of plant pots looked as though they'd need just one tiny push to topple over. On the other side of the greenhouse, yellow tipped leaves of the tomato plants drooped above pots full of dried out compost coming away from their sides. And this was only the beginning of spring. Mum looked lost in the midst of all the garden paraphernalia; a tiny figure attempting to exert some control over the rows of seedlings waiting to be pricked out. A shaft of buttery spring light showed up the wiry grey hair that now framed her face and the flaky skin around nails she used to spend a fortune on a few short months ago. She'd started to let herself go. I just hadn't noticed in between all the 'what ifs', 'if onlys' and disappointing exam results.

So I decided to plunge straight in.

"Can I give you a hand, mum?"

Mum pointedly avoided my offer, focusing instead on a frantic search for a tool to start pricking out tiny cucumber seedlings in the row of seed trays in front of her. It was as if I'd suddenly dissolved in the foetid atmosphere of the tiny greenhouse.

"Is there something wrong? I'm just trying to help."

This time mum slammed the knife down hard on the wooden slats causing one of the towering pots to collapse all over the thicket of tiny seedlings.

"Help? ... Help? *You?*"

"Yeah, why not?"

Now it was mum's turn to laugh, but it wasn't the kind of jocular exchange that made you feel warm inside. Instead, it felt like she'd plunged the dibber she'd managed to locate straight through the sliver of self-esteem that survived the string of disappointing A-level results that had preceded the failed driving test.

"Because ... you never seem to do anything. Make a decision or take the initiative? You? ... I don't know. I thought that was what this gap year was all about. To give you time to pass your driving test without the distraction of A-levels. What was that about? Others seem to manage it. I mean look at Katy..."

Mum was at a loss. She'd chucked the dibber to one side and now lacked the means to assert the much-vaunted sense of purpose she'd championed at every opportunity since I'd failed to live up to the aspirations she'd nurtured ever since I was born.

"That's not entirely true, is it?"

"Oh yes it is! What was this so-called gap year about? Why couldn't you go straight to university or take up one of those start-up schemes like Freya's daughter"

"What, like D-cup-cake-Katy? No wonder she's popular with the punters when they're scoffing their Mediterranean flatbreads down the cultural quarter. Something to sweeten up the day, sir?"

"Oh, that's right. Make fun of her, why don't you? At least she's doing something..."

"What's this really about Mum? I mean *you* don't seem to be achieving a great deal here or elsewhere, do you?"

I'm surprised the neighbours didn't hear the firecracker slap that sent me reeling through the greenhouse door, landing right next to the trowel mum had discarded before she entered the greenhouse. This presented mum with a dilemma. Should she stay and show some concern for me, or should she just cling on to her pride and carry on as if nothing had happened?

She chose the latter course of action. Of course, she did. Well, very nearly. Instead of choosing to help me, she marched straight off into the kitchen to pour herself another glass of Sauvignon Blanc well before the usual 5.00 pm deadline. After about ten minutes spent contemplating the garden from a sedentary position, I returned to the greenhouse, picking my way through the terracotta shards and plastic plant pots to finish the job mum had started or, as she would put it, 'the job in hand'. In what seemed to be a miraculously short period of time, I cleared the floor of debris, washed out the seed trays and put the plant pots into neat columns in the nearby shed. I then proceeded to lift the tiny seedlings out of the tray and into tiny individual pots that would eventually deliver the sleek, green baby cucumbers that mum sliced into her salads. I repotted the tomato plants, sinking their shrivelled roots into crumbly brown compost, doused them in water and put them in an orderly line on the floor of the greenhouse. The tiny star-like flowers would be bearing fat, red, smooth-skinned tomatoes in no time. They'd be ready just before I left for uni.

With that job done, it was time to tackle mum.

All Dead All Gone

Bob Mynors

'End the call now,' Andrew told himself. He did, and then he paused. "Dead?" He spoke the word out loud, almost with a tear. "She can't be."

He had just been talking to Ryan, his nephew. "It's Mum. I found her - in bed - this morning." The catch in his voice obviously meant that what was coming next would not be good news. "She's – she's died."

Ryan's mum was Rita, Andrew's sister, his younger sister. Had Ryan just told him she had been found dead in her bed that morning?

Nick, Ryan's father, had not been there. 'Of course he hadn't,' Andrew thought. 'They've been separated about three months now. Why would he be?' How much that had contributed to Rita's death he didn't dare speculate. But he knew Ryan often called to see his mother on his way to work, so that was how she had been found

Andrew sat down and, finally, was able to take his eyes away from the phone. Ryan was a solicitor, well-used to dealing with people in extreme emotional states. 'But it is always different when it is your own emotions,' Andrew thought. His phone was back in his pocket: still the news had not sunk in. "She can't be dead." What bothered him - what bothered him most, to his immediate shame - was the loss this represented for him, the loss of the last link he had to his past, to a large part of his past, to his family. It didn't leave him without family who belonged to now: he had children, grown-up, and grandchildren. He even had a couple of half-sisters and a half-brother from his father's second marriage, though he never saw them these days. And there was Ryan. But the family he grew up with – parents, grandparents, sister, brothers - they were all dead now, all gone. That book had closed firmly, leaving only memories

Rita hadn't sounded good when they spoke on the phone days earlier. Her voice had been thin, weak. He had considered going to see her at the time. He should have got off his backside and done it. But now it was too late. Now she was past tense like all the others

Their family had been an unfortunate one, fated from the outset. When Andrew's father had told his own parents he wanted to get married at the age of just seventeen, they had disapproved and refused permission: this was not long after the end of the war – World War II. But they had been left with no options when Andrew's mother became pregnant. Andrew was the oldest child, the fruit of that frowned-upon liaison, born not quite seven months after his parents' hurried wedding. Barely a year later, Gerald, a second son, was born, though he had lived for only for six weeks. No-one ever told Andrew the reason for his brother's early death. He was sure he must have asked, but that was probably when he was considered still too young to deal with such information. Had they fobbed him off with *Jesus wanted him to join the choir of angels*, or some such story? It would be like them if they had, though he couldn't honestly remember anything of the sort

They had been more forthcoming when, five years later, his mother had died. Another brother, Brian, and his sister had been born in the intervening period, and his mother's death followed Rita's birth by just three months. In later years, he remembered being told that his mother had suffered with rheumatic fever as a child, which had left her heart weakened and led ultimately to er death – doubtless aided by the final pregnancy. At the time of her death, his memory – he thought it was memory, not fantasy – had him standing in their living room whilst people passed back and forth through the house as he just looked on, his dad at his side

"I won't go and see my mummy," his memory told him he had said

"No. That wouldn't be a good idea," his dad seemed to have replied

"It's not nice for little children to see dead people, is it?"

No response from his dad was ever part of this memory

He always felt this was the moment when they had first appeared in his life. They? The *ghosts*. Not real ghosts – he never claimed a ghost at the foot of his bed or floating up the stairs or anything. He never claimed anything because he was afraid people would laugh. But it did feel that Gerald and his mummy were there, still there, watching him. And whilst he never thought they actually spoke to him, he was sure that he knew what they wanted him to know, wanted him to do

There were times soon afterwards when he just got up and walked out of school. He was sure someone must have told him to do this, and who but his mummy or Gerald would have done that? It was not a sensible thing to do, he knew. It worried the school too, but they knew what he had been through, and they were kind, whilst trying to find a way to deal with the situation. He always went straight home – or rather to the house next door to home, the house where Auntie Rose and Uncle Percy lived. They weren't his real auntie and uncle, but they did look after him in the morning when his daddy went to work and before he went to school, and after school until his daddy got home. Sometimes he did think he knew mummy and Gerald had wanted him to go home – like the day when Auntie Rose was trying to do some sewing but had dropped her reel of cotton. Auntie Rose was very short-sighted, and Uncle Percy was completely blind. When Andrew walked into their house, his auntie was on her knees under the kitchen table and his uncle was shouting from the living room, asking where she was - but she wasn't answering

Once Andrew had understood the situation, young though he was, he was able to tell his uncle that his auntie was looking for something, and then he just dropped to the floor and, within seconds, had found the dropped reel. His auntie was relieved, and she gave him a soppy kiss. His uncle was more concerned about why he had walked out of school – this was not the first time it had happened – but he didn't seem cross – just concerned. Andrew just knew his mummy would be smiling at what he had done. She would think he had been very kind and would be pleased with him

She helped him too, he thought, and Gerald did, when he needed them. There was the night when he woke up and he could hear rain beating against his window. When he opened his eyes, he could see – thought he could see - a little man running up and down the outside of his window, trying to get inside. He couldn't actually see the man: he could see a shadow of a man running up and down the side of the building outside the window. Andrew was frightened. He wanted to cry. He wanted to call out for someone – there was only his daddy. But then he suddenly felt calm. He knew there were no men as small as the one he saw– smaller than a baby. And anyone who tried to run up and down the wall outside his window would fall to the ground. He didn't know that these things were told to him by Gerald, his brother, the brother he hadn't known. But he said a relieved thank you, just in case

Years passed, until the day came when his grandad died. Grandad, his father's father, was his only grandfather. No contact existed now with his mother's family, but her spirit had never let it be known to him that this bothered her. Grandad had always seemed, and continued to seem, even decades later, the wisest and wittiest man Andrew ever knew – almost a storybook grandfather except that he didn't have the white beard. Whenever later in life Andrew solved some issue, or when he came up with a joke that people really laughed at, he thought of Grandad and knew his guiding hand was involved somewhere, somehow. Andrew was glad to have known Grandad, if only for the dozen or so years of life they had shared

Brian, his younger brother, was a different kettle. In age, just two years and seven months separated them – and there was Gerald between. Whilst Andrew had always been a tolerably well-behaved child, achieving anything he did achieve quietly, Brian was anything but. Unruly when young, he grew into a thug and a criminal. More than one period of his life was spent in prison. Behind him, he left a trail of nine children – nine that Andrew knew of – by five women

"What do you want?" Andrew asked one night when Brian turned up on the doorstep, unannounced, having not been seen or of heard for months

"Not eaten all day. What yer got?"

Andrew shrugged and let him in. He was pretty confident that, if he were the hungry one, his brother would have little sympathy, but he opened the freezer and offered a choice. "You won't mind if I take some of these with me, will you?" Brian said

Andrew knew that his wife would mind immensely, but she was at her sister's. He should be able to get Brian out of the way before she came home. At least the kids were in bed and would have nothing to tell her when they saw her in the morning. They didn't need to, of course. When, next morning, everyone was getting ready for school or work, their younger son's little voice piped up, "Where's my money box?"

A quick and frantic search began, fruitless as Andrew knew it would be. He owned up that Brian had been round the night before. Not only had his brother cleared out nearly half the contents of their freezer, but he had also stolen their son's money box. There had been maybe forty pounds in it – money that Andrew would have to make up: he would not be going to the pub much in the coming weeks

Again, years passed as they inexorably do. Brian moved to live in another city. Andrew heard little more of him, until the day a girl Andrew remembered fondly from junior school contacted him via Facebook and invited him to a sort of school reunion celebrating the year that his class group turned fifty. One of the boys he used to play with but hadn't seen since the day they all left and went to different schools, said to him, "I was sorry to hear about your Brian."

Andrew thought about trying to bluff, then thought better of it. "What have you heard?" he asked, expecting another prison sentence or something. His jaw must have hit the floor when he heard the word *dead*. How convincingly he concealed his feelings, he could not know. They were a mix of relief, shame at the years of separation and trepidation about the disturbance Brian might cause from beyond the grave. The cosy relationship he enjoyed with those already watching over him was surely about to change. 'That's just guilty conscience,' he told himself. But he didn't believe it

It didn't take long for him to start feeling oppressed by memories of occasions when he had perhaps been unfair to his brother. 'That really is just guilty conscience.' He tried to counter such memories with thoughts of the times when his brother had been unfair – or worse – to him. Uppermost amongst them was the time when, after his thirteen-year-old self had spent a whole Saturday afternoon reading up on Anglo-Saxon life in Britain, then writing what felt like an incredibly long essay on the subject, Andrew had found his exercise book the next morning with bright red wax crayon marks all over his work. Not only did he have to copy it out again, but he also had to plead for mercy from his history teacher – and receive a whacking

The expected onslaught never arrived though. Perhaps Grandad, the only grown-up who had ever really connected with Brian during childhood, was working the same magic, or perhaps Brian was finally enjoying the mother-love he had lacked as a child. Whatever the cause, Andrew continued to feel only warmth from what he assumed was *the other side*

If this meant only that he was learning to go easy on himself, it was welcome. It didn't last for long though. Soon afterwards, a thought struck him or a suggestion was made to him – he didn't know which. He became obsessed with the question of what would happen to his *ghosts* as he thought of them - even called them on occasions when he dared speak of them - after he had gone, after he was no longer there to remember. Perhaps it was his fast-approaching sixtieth birthday and thoughts of his own mortality. Perhaps his *ghosts* feared the fate that awaited them when his own life was snuffed out. He did his best to shut such thoughts out

After a few more years, Grandma died. Grandma was the woman who had stepped up selflessly to raise three grandchildren as if they had been her own offspring. Her ideas of child-rearing belonged to an earlier generation, but there was no doubting the love she had for all of them, or the pain she felt whenever she was let down by one of them

"I don't know why I put up with you lot," she often complained. "I ought to 'ave you all put in a children's 'ome." Rita didn't like this: it made her cry. But Brian and Andrew used to smirk about it quietly: they knew Grandma better than that

When finally she died, forty-one years after the death of her husband, she continued her complaints, so Andrew thought, from beyond this life. She and Grandad had only recently begun to enjoy their own lives together, free of the ties of parenthood, when these three children had landed in their laps, and suddenly again, Andrew was conscious of her complaints. 'But it wasn't our fault, Grandma,' he would often think. 'You can't blame us for that.' He wasn't convincing anyone, least of all himself. He tried to appeal to his mummy, to Grandad, to intervene. No help seemed to come but, with time, the hurt eased, and again he got on with his life

Another decade passed, then his dad died. Dad had been a sick man for more than thirty years since a cerebral aneurysm had cruelly robbed him of much of what had made his life worth living. He had remarried in mid-life and raised a new family, very similar in age to Andrew's own children. For years, the two families had been close, but when his father suffered his illness, his stepmother began to complain bitterly about what a bad woman Andrew's mother had been. He had heard such stories throughout his life from his father and his grandma. He didn't like the stories then, but at least

88

they came from people who had known his mother
– known her better than he ever had. But hearing
them from his stepmother, who had never even met
his mother, was too much. He simply stopped
visiting. Thus he lost touch with another branch of
his family

Dad's death was another he had learned of late.
Knowing the poor state of his father's health, he
would sometimes check death notices online. One
day, four months after the event, he found the news
he had been looking for, had been dreading. His
father was dead. At least his father could be
reunited with his parents, with his second son, but
also with his first wife. That could be an interesting
reunion

Still Andrew was thinking about what happens to
the memories, to the spirits, the ghosts of the people
he had known and lost. On the one hand, he had no
time for theories of afterlife and spirits, of heaven
and hell. On the other, he still felt connected to all
the people he had lost. And now he had lost one
more. He had lost Rita who was, part of him felt
sure, now reunited with her grandparents, with her
father, with the mother she had never known and
with two of her brothers. Would she change the

relationship he had with those who had died before her? Would any changes be for better or for worse?

◊

Andrew woke with a pain in his chest, a serious pain, a pain like a horse was inside his chest trying to kick its way out through the back of his ribcage. It was a pain that was all too familiar. It was a heart attack, he knew: he had already had two in his life. He managed to find his phone and dial 999, then croak his name and address, and his inexpert diagnosis, down the phone. The operator sprang into action, though it still felt like forever before an ambulance crew began beating on his door. He had had enough time to throw pants, t-shirts and a few hankies into a bag. He threw his phone and a charger in too. Just before the hammering on his door started, he thought to pick up the tray in which he kept his medications: they would thank him for that at the hospital, he was sure

The paramedic attaching electrodes to his chest once they were inside the ambulance said it probably would not have mattered, but eventually managed to compliment his quick-thinking. Twice during the ride, the ambulance used its siren and, despite his condition, he managed to feel a thrill at this

Outside the hospital, there was a wait: he had no idea how long, but the horse was still kicking away inside him. Eventually though, they got him inside the hospital, on to a trolley and into a side room. Nurses fussed round him – temperature and blood pressure checks, identity checks, fixing a bracelet round his wrist, attaching him to a drip, lots more questions, injections in his stomach, and questions, questions. All the while, they were watching him – the *ghosts* – Grandma and Grandad, mummy and daddy, his sister and his brothers. Were they watching over him or were they welcoming him? He didn't know. He couldn't know. He was tired. The horse seemed to have tired too. It was no longer kicking as hard

One of the nurses had taken his phone and rung his sons to let them know where he was. In what felt like no time, no time compared to his earlier waits, they were at the side of his bed, one with his partner. The wife of his other son, a childminder, was not able to get away. The three of them stared down at him with big, sorrowful, almost cartoon eyes.

Somehow, he found the strength to speak. "I'm going," he said. "I'm going back."

"Don't talk, dad," his younger son said

"No, don't talk," said the older. "Save your strength."

He ignored them. "I'm going back." His voice was weak but there were things he needed to say. "There's no more. There's no after, no next. We're all just dust going back to the Earth. We're all just atoms going back to the universe. I'm going …"

The Silent Man

Neil McGill

Before the car came to a halt on the drive, I knew it was him. The aged figure occupying the back seat of the car had baleful blue eyes, lank grey hair, it was him. Even as the Detective Inspector introduced him as Professor Steven Longley, an academic with whom the FBI had consulted on occasion, I knew it was him. The silent man got out of the car, looking quite sprightly for a man in his eighties. He was tall and lean with an enquiring demeanour.

Gerald had told me to be wary if this guy ever turned up. He had said, "He says little, but sees and hears everything."

The Inspector dismissed his driver after I had said that there was no need for a WPC to be present, that this was all informal and that I felt at ease in my own home. I led the way into the kitchen diner and asked my visitors to sit where they may. The silent man perched himself on a bar stool, where he sat motionless, legs crossed, elbow on the island with his jaw cupped in his hand and his other hand ferreting about for something in his coat pocket. The Inspector and I had occupied the two small couches. I'd purchased couches rather than individual armchairs to give the kitchen diner an informal, colourful, comfortable feel. However, with hindsight and with the silent man peering down on us from his elevated position, I wished I had plumped for a couch and two armchairs instead.

The Inspector explained that the elderly gentleman, Professor Longley, was here essentially to observe, but that he may have questions to help determine whether the person he sought and my visitor were one and the same. As the Inspector spoke emphasising the seriousness of the matter, the silent man had taken from his pocket a hard boiled sweet which he was slowly and meticulously unwrapping. The Inspector said that much had changed since our phone call some weeks earlier and what had seemed almost a trivial school break-in back in twenty nineteen had now escalated into a matter that may have wider implications.

Detective Inspector Tudor was quite short for a policeman, dark haired, brown eyed, probably about fifty. A cold, detached, professional air emanated from him. No-one could imagine him being the heart and soul of the party. He spoke with an almost monotone voice which is perhaps why my gaze was constantly being drawn to the silent man, who at this time was sucking on his sweet whilst studying the fridge magnets, twisting and knotting the sweet wrapper between his fingers.

"This is a serious matter, Mrs O'Neil," a rebuke from the Inspector for my lack of attention. "You may be implicated in a criminal conspiracy. Your visitor of October twenty nineteen apparently hacked into several government agencies here and abroad at roughly the same time as you were entertaining him here in your home."

I was momentarily stunned by this announcement. "Do I need legal representation?" I thought. But before I could say the words, the Inspector backtracked, apologising for his words saying, "I'm sorry. That was inappropriate. You're not a suspect. Indeed, I believe any involvement of yours to be totally innocent and of minor consequence. But we do have to establish the facts." He paused for a moment. "If you feel you need a friend present, we can arrange to speak with you again on another occasion."

I looked over at the silent man, his eyes had not shifted from the fridge magnets, and he projected an air of total disinterest, although I doubt he missed a single word of what had been said. I turned back to the Inspector and, in an aggrieved voice, said, "When you phoned you said that this was going to be an informal chat, an information gathering session. I didn't expect to be treated like I was under investigation."

The expression on the Inspector's face was of a man genuinely troubled by his own words. "Mrs O'Neil, I can only apologise again." There was a short pause. "You see, you're the only person in the village who has been able to supply a consistent description, the only person to have spoken with the suspect, the only person who can supply any insight. In truth, we need your help if we are to be able to find this man."

A moment passed, the Inspector glanced over at the silent man whose attention now was taken by the garden beyond the kitchen window; I went across to the patio doors feigning nervous indecision whilst all the while watching the Inspector's reactions reflected in the window.

The morning rain was subsiding and, here and there, wee patches of blue had begun to break through the clouds. I occupied myself straightening the curtains in their ties and then said, without turning, "It's been nearly twelve years since my husband passed and, in all that time, I've had to make my own decisions. It's been ever so lonely. Oh, I have friends who visit and I have my pastimes, but it's not the same. Those few days in the company of Gerald, my mysterious visitor, helped me through a bad patch, helped to reboot my life, gave me purpose, and brought a smile back to my face. He is, was, one of those positive people you meet so seldom in life, but they leave you with a warm smile inside whenever you think of them."

I turned towards the Inspector and the silent man. "I think we can continue as we are."

"I've known personal loss myself," said the Inspector "It can be debilitating, but I can assure you of my intentions, and I have only your safety and best interests at heart." The silent man, still seated, was now looking directly at me; he gave the slightest nod of agreement.

"Right," I said, feeling quite assertive, "if we are going to continue this conversation, I insist we do it with a hot drink in front of us. Would you like tea or coffee?"

I skirted past the silent man who made no attempt to move his long legs out of my way. I filled the kettle and turned it on. "So what will it be, gentlemen"?

It was the silent man who spoke first. "Tea, white, two sugars." His American accent was so familiar. I thought southern states, Mississippi, Texas perhaps, and then the film The Fugitive came into my mind, the good cop who played opposite Harrison Ford's character, his name I couldn't remember but it was the same sounding voice.

The Inspector said, "Same for me, but no sugar, please."

As I looked in the press, the Inspector started to recall our telephone conversation. "You said that your visitor was approximately mid-sixties, five foot ten, dark hair, greying rapidly, dark blue eyes. You went on to say that he gave the name Gerald Anderson, but you believe that to be an alias. He seemed fit, weighed in the region of 12 stone, with no tattoos or distinguishing marks."

"That's correct. Cups or mugs?"

"I think mugs will be fine," answered the Inspector. "Did he have a noticeable accent?"

"Well he had a kind of American accent but not one I could place, and at times he sounded different, as if he might be putting it on. Strong or weak? Your tea, I mean."

"You can leave the tea bag in for me," was the Inspector's response.

The silent man thought for a moment and then said, "Weak."

"Now you also said that on each occasion you met, he wore the same hiking clothes, blue knee length coat with hood, denim trousers and hiking boots or shoes, but you don't recall any brand names."

"Yes, that's correct, although he was wearing a suit when we met at the airport hotel."

"Airport hotel? "You had met previously"?

"Well, yes, well I'd met him twice previous to the last time in October twenty nineteen. I'm sorry. I'm not explaining this very well, am I?"

"You never mentioned meeting him before when we spoke on the phone."

"Yes, but when we spoke on the phone you were making enquiries about the school break-in. I didn't relate that to the earlier meetings. Please give me a moment to collect my thoughts." I closed my eyes for a moment and then breathed in and out heavily through my nose.

I placed the sugar bowl and a mug of weak tea in front of the silent man. "Help yourself if it isn't sweet enough." I then handed a mug to the Inspector, who was still sitting down, and I sat down on the couch opposite. I stared for a moment into the mug of tea between my hands then, realising it was actually burning me through the porcelain, I put it down on the coffee table in front of me.

"Perhaps it would be better to start again but this time from the very beginning," I said

The Inspector, who for the first time had the foundations of a smile upon his face, nodded and said, "Perhaps."

I leaned back on the couch and drew a cushion up close to myself. The silent man was doing what I've seen other old folk do, that is drinking his tea from the teaspoon as if it were soup.

"About a year earlier, that would be twenty eighteen and around the same time, late October early November. The country had been lashed with Atlantic storms. The storms had downed electric supply cables and the greater part of Western Scotland was without power. Here in the Borders, there had been less in the way of power outages, but there were some fallen trees and minor disruptions to supply. So when a knock came to the door about six or seven o'clock in the evening, I naturally assumed it was one of the council workers checking to see if people in the remoter parts of the community had heat and lighting. It was a dreadful night so I invited the man into the kitchen. It was the old kitchen, before I'd had it converted.

"'Come in, come in,' I said. 'I can't leave you out there in this weather; I didn't hear your truck pulling up.'

"'No, no I walked here,' he said.

"'Walked all the way from the village? Are the roads closed? Well you're going to have a warm

101

drink and a wee bit of something inside you before you go back out there.'

"The man had an impish smile on his face. 'I think we are at cross purposes. I'm looking to speak to Lesley Anne Bywater. I believe she lives here.'

"'Aunt Lesley! She passed away many years ago. Whatever could you want with her?'

"With some confusion in his eyes, he asked, 'Has she been dead long? You see, I got this book.' He bent over and extracted it from his rucksack. 'It says on the inside cover that she had retired from her role as a criminal psychologist, and planned to spend her days writing short stories for local publications and tending her garden here in Balstrie.'

"At this point I think I should explain something." I looked at the Inspector, but then noticed the curious look on the silent man's face. "I should explain that some years ago, after my husband passed, I tried to immerse myself in various pastimes and projects. One of them was the local book club. I'd been reading historical dramas and, when someone suggested that we all should have a go at writing something ourselves, I thought I'd give it a go. My short story was well received by the group, with a couple suggesting I should have it published, so I did. But when the publishers asked for a bio, I thought about my aunt. She had raised me when my mother died. My father was in a new relationship and, as an eleven-year-old, I became difficult and very unhappy. My aunt scooped me up from London and brought me here. At that age I hadn't even been sure that I had an aunt. Mom and Dad rarely spoke of her, but once we met, there was instant chemistry. I fell in love with her and with this place. When my husband passed in twenty eleven, she insisted that I move back in here with her, and we had two years of looking after each other until her death in twenty thirteen. So, when it came to the bio for the book, I sent her name and details as homage to her memory.

"When I related what I've just told you to my visitor, he seemed moved by the news of my aunt's death, and a little dejected, but then he asked what I thought to be a very weird, personal and insensitive question'? 'I suppose your aunt didn't leave any diaries or reports from her time as a psychologist.' I went from zero to boiling in an instant; I used profanities the like of which I've never used before. I ordered him out of the house and told him I would be phoning the police.

"Then … It came to me. 'You're after the f___ing Merlin Chutes, aren't you? Where are you from? The newspapers?'

"My rage scared the life out of him, and he was out the door in an instant but, just as I went to close and bolt the door, he stepped back inside momentarily. Speaking in a calm voice, he said, 'I'm very sorry to have upset you in this way. It was never my intention. By all means phone the police if you feel at all threatened, but for both our sakes, I wouldn't mention that you know anything about the Merlin Chutes.' With that, he disappeared into the night."

The Inspector jumped in with an immediate question. "Did you notify the police"?

"No. After a few minutes, I calmed down and, when I thought about it, I asked myself what could they do? I'd invited him in. He hadn't touched or threatened me and, with the night being as bad as it was, they probably had better things to be doing."

Then there was that voice again as the silent man put in his two pennyworth. "As a criminal psychologist, your aunt, I imagine, would have kept extensive notes and diaries of her patients. Are they still available?"

"No," I told him. "There's nothing, she kept nothing." I thought for a moment. "She did say that at some of the places she went to, the security was so tight that she was searched when entering and when leaving, and that all notes, recordings, reports and the like had to remain in the building. It became very difficult to do her job properly. I think that's how she fell foul of her bosses."

"When you say she 'fell foul of her bosses', what exactly does that mean?" the Inspector asked.

I had been trying to skirt around this chapter of my aunt's life. She was a wonderful, witty, intelligent person who wouldn't harm a fly, and I knew this revelation could only tarnish her image in their eyes. "They accused her of passing on personal details of some of her clients to the media."

The Inspector's eyes narrowed slightly. "For cash?"

"No, nothing like that. It never happened. It was just an excuse to get rid of her and blacken her character. The stress caused by the accusation caused her to have a severe breakdown and she had to be hospitalised. I think that's why my parents never mentioned her, due to the embarrassment."

The Inspector spoke in a conciliatory tone. "I would have thought her family would have stood by her at a time like that. I mean, that would have been the seventies, eighties, I'm guessing. But I suppose attitudes back then to mental health issues might have been different."

"Some years later, she received a full apology and compensation from her employers. She used the money to buy this place." I felt I had to get that in, in defence of my aunt.

You could see in the Inspector's eyes that my answers had created a thousand new questions. "So, let me get this right. A man you had never previously met knocks on your door on a stormy autumn night asking to see your aunt who had been dead for about five years. He then asks if your aunt had left any diaries or reports. And you, in response, accuse him of being from the media and wanting the Merlin Chutes. What are the Merlin Chutes, Mrs O'Neil?"

"Inspector, please." The silent man had come to my rescue. "Give the lady a moment to draw breath. Remember, this is not an interrogation. We're here merely to establish a timeline and the facts about this 'Gerald Anderson'. By the way,

Inspector, why did you say earlier that you thought he was using an alias?"

The Inspector looked like he'd just been slapped in the face. He had a questioning expression, as he looked daggers at the older man. Then, sitting back on the couch and recovering his composure ever so slowly, he turned to me. "I'm very sorry, Mrs O'Neil. I was forgetting myself. This gentleman is very correct. I'm racing on. It's a habit I've picked up in this job and I really should work on it."

"Whilst I've been sitting in this lofty perch, I couldn't help noticing a delightful smell in the room, the kind of smell I recall from my mother's kitchen when I was just a whippersnapper. Now you wouldn't have been doing a bit of baking recently, would you?" The silent man spoke with the cheekiest glint in his eyes. He had clearly enjoyed the Inspector's question and answer session, but had not wanted the Inspector to tackle the elephant in the room, the Merlin Chutes. I knew why, of course, the silent man knew far more about the Merlin Chutes than me, or anybody else on the planet.

"I don't think it's baking you're smelling, Professor, I think your nose has caught a whiff of the hash that's on the stove," I said.

"Hash?" The silent man looked at the Inspector for clarification.

"A kind of stew made with corned beef or mince with vegetables and potatoes. Very fortifying."

"Would you like a bowl, Professor?" I asked. His eyes grew big and his smile widened into a grin.

"Sure. I'd love that."

"And you, Inspector?"

Looking at the clock above the hearth, he said, "As long as it's not robbing you of your dinner."

It wasn't, I assured him. I'd made enough to last a couple of days.

As I went to put the heat under the pot, the silent man stood and, leaning towards me, said, in a low voice, almost a whisper, "Could you direct me to the restroom?"

I directed him through the door to the stairs and said, "Top of the stairs, first right." Then, realising his age, I said, "There's a downstairs lavvy in the hall where you came in if that would be better."

"No, this will be fine. It's the plumbing not the legs that don't work so well," was his reply.

As I turned back to the kitchen, it dawned on me that I'd given this man, of whom I had been suspicious from the beginning, access to the whole house. But within a minute or so I heard the cistern flush, and he was back in the kitchen.

"Fine house you have here. Three bedrooms?"

"No," I said, "four, but one I use as a bit an office."

"You have some grand views, very tranquil; your aunt picked a nice spot."

The Inspector, who had been sitting in total silence for a few minutes, interrupted with, "The name Gerald Anderson, very similar to Gerry Anderson, the creator of children's sci-fi fantasy. He and his wife produced animated TV programmes in the Sixties and Seventies."

The silent man looked puzzled and, palming his thinning grey hair down to his collar, asked, "And the relevance is?"

"You asked why the lady thought it was an alias."

Turning up his bottom lip and nodding ever so slowly, the silent man said, "I did, didn't I?"

I couldn't tell why, but I felt the Inspector had just asked a very calculated question. The silent man held the Inspector's gaze for what seemed like an eternity. "It might be more comfortable if we all sat around the island to eat," I said.

The Inspector broke his stare and turned his eyes towards me. With that shadow of a smile he'd used earlier, he said, "That's fine."

We sat and ate; there was little conversation, the occasional remark about the contents of the hash or the flavour: I like to add a little chilli to the mix. As we sat there, the impression began to develop in my mind that these two had no liking for each other, that fate had thrown them together, but fate was responsible for a complete mismatch. The Inspector was stiff, formal, impatient, whilst the silent man, contrary to my initial impression, was calm, relaxed and the very model of patience. But then I wondered whether they were just playing good cop, bad cop.

The Inspector broke the tranquillity of my thoughts, whilst the silent man was still chasing the last bit of carrot and gravy around the bowl. He said, "I need to tackle the matter of your meeting at the airport hotel. Which airport would that be?"

"Glasgow."

"And the hotel?"

"The Meridian."

"And can you tell me about the circumstances of your meeting with Gerald Anderson?"

"Would you like more tea before I start, as this could be a long time in the telling?" I said.

The Inspector shook his head and looked at the silent man. The silent man looked at me and said, "I'm fine."

"Well, it's like this," I said. "In July, after that first meeting, my friend and I were preparing for our holiday in the Canaries. We try to go every year at the beginning of the summer break. We both work as support staff at the school; I only do a couple of days. Well, on the morning we were to drive to Glasgow, I received a phone call. At first, I thought it was Stacy, phoning to tell me she'd lost her passport or something; anxiety should be her middle name."

"Landline or mobile?" the Inspector asked.

"That would have been …" and I had to think for a moment, "… the mobile. "Definitely the mobile, because I remember thinking afterwards, 'How had he got my number?'"

The Inspector raised his eyes and glanced at the silent man. The silent man caught his glance and just nodded.

"Well, as you will have guessed, it was the man who had called here six, eight months previously. Before I even got the chance to speak, he asked me not to hang up. He then apologised for his … how did he put it? … his blundering, insensitive and ill-prepared intrusion into my life. There was sincerity in his voice and even remorse. He went on to explain that he didn't work for the media or any government agency, and that his interest in my aunt's work was purely based on professional curiosity. He continued saying that he knew of my aunt's work and held the belief that her troubles with her employer had stemmed from inadvertently stumbling upon a classified military project.

"I was actually speechless, probably for the first time in my life. He asked me, 'Are you still there? Are you alright?'

"I finally answered 'Why?'

"'Why?' he came back.

"'Yes, why?' I said. 'Why are you telling me this?'

"'Well,' he went on. 'I think it could be mutually beneficial if we could meet up and discuss your aunt's work.'

"'I still don't understand why. Why, after all this time, you're wanting to rake up all this stuff about my aunt and what you think I could tell you. I was a child when all this happened.'

"For a couple of seconds, although it felt like a couple of minutes, there was silence. Then a sigh, and then he spoke. 'In the nineteen eighties, I was involved with a group researching particle physics in the US. Accusations were made that I had been involved with the transfer of information to a third party. Although there was no evidence to corroborate the accusation my position was terminated.

"'I was aggrieved by what had happened, but I dusted myself off and came to Britain to start a new role. It was some seventeen months later that I heard there had been an explosion and fire at the facility in the US, and many good people had died. From that day to this, the circumstances surrounding my termination and the subsequent explosion and fire have troubled me.

"'Then, by chance, in twenty eighteen, almost four decades after the events I have just spoken of, I was looking at a collection of books kept by the hotel I was staying in. Books that had been left or donated by guests, and there amongst them was a copy of *Lady of Rochelle* by Lesley Anne Bywater. Immediately memories of the name came flooding back to me: Lesley Anne Bywater was the name of the third party - the third party I was accused of passing information to all those years ago. So you can imagine my desire to meet her and to find out what she knew. She obviously spoke to you about it. How else could you have known about what you said to me that night?'

"I told him that my aunt had told me very little of her work. It was in the past and she didn't like talking about it. On the rare occasions she did mention it, she would tell me, if anybody came nosing about, asking questions about her or her work, tell them nothing, and in fact tell them to f… off.

"The bit about the Merlin Chutes? She didn't really tell me that. It was towards the end, when she was on strong medication which at times made her delirious, and it was during those outbursts that she would say, 'Don't say. Don't tell them about the Merlin Chutes.' On other occasions she might scream, 'Hide. Kill.' or 'Don't let them find the Merlin Chutes,' or shout out the names of people she had known and point them out as if they were in the room. So, you see, I don't really know anything about the Merlin Chutes except that the very thought of them terrified my aunt.

"Persistently, Gerald said, 'I still think we should meet. There's much I'd like to tell you that I can't say over the phone.'

"I said, 'Even if I agreed to meet you, it couldn't be for several weeks as we've got a holiday booked and will fly out in the morning.'

"His response was, 'Can I call to see you this evening? I won't take up more than an hour of your time. It is important.'

"I said, 'We are driving up to Glasgow this afternoon, so it won't be possible.'

"I heard him say to himself 'Glasgow.' Then there was a pause, and then I heard, 'It is possible. Look,' he said, 'could I meet up with you and your friend in Glasgow? I could buy you both dinner.'

"I eventually agreed and we met in the hotel restaurant."

The Inspector rubbed his eyes and pinched his nose with the thumb and forefinger of his right hand and, without looking up, said, "You told a complete stranger that your house would be empty for a couple of weeks. Was that wise?"

I just gave him an embarrassed smile and asked, "Are you sure you don't want anything to drink?"

The Inspector continued. "The Merlin Chutes, I know you have said you have no knowledge of them, but didn't this Gerald give you the slightest inkling of what it was all about?"

Before I could answer, the silent man interrupted. This time he said, "I have my own ideas about the Merlin Chutes, Inspector. Perhaps I can share them with you later. At the moment, I'd rather hear what the lady has to say about her meeting at the restaurant."

The Inspector straightened himself in his seat, a look of satisfaction on his face; he had expected the silent man would divert his line of questioning. Then, looking me in the eyes, he said, "Please continue."

I had given up on trying to work out what game these two guys were playing, so I explained that I had told my friend Stacy that an old acquaintance had phoned, and that he had offered to buy us both dinner. He was in town on business, I told her, and might not get the chance to see me again for some time. Stacy asked lots of questions of course. My answers were coyishly vague. She got it into her head that it was some old flame, even after I told her I hardly knew the man.

"We were about ten minutes late arriving at the restaurant; Gerald was there ahead of us. We sat down and made pleasant conversation. Gerald explained that he was on a stopover; his connecting flight to Berlin had been rescheduled and he couldn't think of any better way to spend the time than in the company of two young ladies. Stacy couldn't help herself, of course, and asked how long we had known each other. Gerald replied, 'Not too long. We had what you might call a brief encounter a few months ago.'

"Stacy gave me that knowing look; I gave her the look that said, 'Cut it out.'

"We ordered our meals; the menu was a bit pricey but the quality was excellent. We had two courses and a couple of glasses of wine apiece, and then Stacy said she had some last minute shopping to do. She told Gerald that it was nice to have met him and thanked him for the meal, and said that she'd meet me back in the room later.

"Gerald asked, 'Would you like tea or coffee?' We both had tea. The confident, self-assured Gerald of a couple of minutes earlier had given way to a less confident, almost anxious Gerald as he said it was important that he saw me as soon as possible, and before his flight to Berlin. He explained that, since our earlier heated meeting, he had encountered some strange coincidences that had made him reassess what he thought he knew. He didn't elaborate on the coincidences but said, 'I have a proposition for you. I have always thought to leave a record of what happened back in the eighties, initially as testimony to those who died. But now I'm thinking that perhaps it would be prudent to involve a wider circle of people, people with special knowledge or insight of those events. But here's the rub. I'm a little low on trust when it comes to those people. So here's my proposition. I will tell you my story, a story that in the main will be fiction, but with enough parallels for those special people to be able to join the dots. You will write my story. You have the time and the skills, and you can have total control over it. You can cut, carve, re-assemble, add or subtract. If it sells, you'll take full credit for it: if it flops you can say some crazy guy gave you the story. Either way you will be a lot closer to understanding your aunt's part in it all.'

"I gave myself a moment to digest it all, and then said to him, 'But why don't you write it? And why the subterfuge?'

"'It's about trust,' he said. 'Back in the eighties, the leader of the project, an incredibly gifted individual and scientist, had said that if anything were ever to go wrong, my dismissal may prove invaluable. I would be outside the project, but my knowledge of the facilities and personnel would make me the go-to person in the case of an investigation. I would also be able to transmit the concerns that he and the other leading scientists had regarding the morality and safety of the research they were undertaking.'

119

"He went on to suggest that there was a cast of characters who, although without links to the project, had the knowledge and expertise to assist in any investigation. However, he had reservations as to how much trust could be placed in all the members of the cast of characters, and that I should exercise extreme caution when dealing with them. 'I don't know if those people will, when armed with the information I will be giving them, use it wisely. Regarding the writing, I've spent the best part of forty years trying to put pen to paper, but I don't have what it takes.'

"We both then spent what seemed like an age before speaking again. He was looking into his teacup trying to discern if the words he had used had been the right ones. I was thinking, 'Do I really want to write someone else's story?' Then, as the thought occurred to me, I said, 'Is there any risk to me in this?'

"He looked at me with hands crossed and study in his eyes. Then, lying back in his seat and rolling his eyes to the ceiling, he said, in a slow, careful voice, 'Use your own name and have it published under fiction. There should be no comebacks. If it works though, you might have people coming to see you, trying to get to me. But I'm certain that's a situation you can deal with.'"

It was at that point the silent man interrupted. He addressed the Inspector, saying, "Inspector Tudor, would you mind giving Mrs O'Neil and myself a few minutes alone? I have a couple of questions I would like to ask in private."

The Inspector's eyes flashed with alarm, looking first at the silent man and then me. "That would be against established protocols, sir. A senior police officer should be in attendance at all times during an interview by a member of an outside agency."

The silent man dipped his hand into his coat pocket as he said, "Don't think of it as an interview Inspector. It's a couple of questions. I don't think the lady will mind."

Inspector Tudor looked at me with genuine concern in his eyes. "I would recommend against it. It's quite irregular."

The silent man had fished yet another of the hard boiled sweets from his pocket and was in the process of unwrapping it as he said, "The lady is quite safe with me, Inspector. I'm hardly a spring chicken." Then, with a mischievous smile, he said,

"Anyways, I had to leave my knuckle dusters with airport security."

With concern still etched on the Inspector's face, I said, "It'll be alright, Inspector. I have a few questions I would like to ask the Professor."

The Inspector's demeanour had changed little; he rose from his seat, turned toward the patio doors and said, "I'll be out in the garden. I will be in view at all times, if you need me." With that, he stepped out into the garden. He immediately took out his mobile phone and began searching for a phone number.

The silent man left his stool and occupied the spot on the couch the Inspector had occupied earlier. "Mrs O'Neil, Gillian, or would you prefer Gill?"

"Gill would be just fine," I said.

He went on, "Please come and sit down here on the couch. The book that the gentleman spoke of, I assume you agreed to write it."

"I did."

He gave an affirmative nod, and then acrobatically moved the hard boiled sweet from one side of his mouth to the other. He continued, "Not been published yet?"

I said "No, it's not complete."

"Hmm, I don't suppose you would allow me to have a look at it?"

"I don't think any writer would want their work read until it's completed," I said, "but I am prepared to read you some extracts from it, if that will help."

The silent man looked out through the glass in the patio doors to where the Inspector appeared to be having a heated conversation on the phone and, with a widening grin, said, "Do you have a title for the book, Gill?"

"The Merlin Chutes".

"And was that your choice or was it this mystery man's choice?"

"It was Gerald's choice; in fact it was the only thing he insisted upon."

The silent man shifted his attention from the Inspector, turning to me and, with big eyes and the broadest of smiles, asked, "And how would you describe your relationship with this man?"

It was a question I had been expecting for some time. "In the short time we were together, we enjoyed each other's company. Beyond that I'd rather not say."

"You have some questions for me?"

"Yes, I have one," and with my hand raised and index finger pointing back across my shoulder to the figure in the garden, I said, "Who is that?"

If it was possible for his broad smile to get broader, then it did, and with the fingers of his left hand circling his mouth, and looking to where I had just pointed, I heard the hard boiled sweet rattle against the inside of his teeth. His left hand moved from his face and he began slowly to massage his left ear lobe, whilst he contemplated a suitable answer. After what seemed an eternity, he simply replied, "I don't know."

"You don't know?"

Looking askance at the Inspector and choosing his words slowly, he said, "The Inspector met me at Heathrow. Your Home Office had notified me in advance that someone would meet me. He was wearing his full dress uniform, looking quite conspicuous. From the off, his manner was abrasive and suspicious. I heard later that he wasn't happy chaperoning some 'geriatric old fart'. For my part, I wasn't any happier, I felt I'd been saddled with a rather pompous twit. When we got to the hotel, I made a few phone calls to see if it would be possible for the Inspector to be assigned to other duties as I felt he would be happier elsewhere."

Here, the silent man paused, then, with a very thoughtful look said, "Within three hours I received a hand-delivered message from the embassy." Again, he paused, and looking out at the Inspector, who by this time had finished his phone call and was looking in at where we sat, said, "The message read along the lines of 'We have the greatest respect and admiration for Detective Inspector Harry Tudor. He can be relied upon to be resourceful and discreet. You will afford him your fullest cooperation. W.H.'

"The White House?" I exclaimed.

"Yes. It would appear that our friend the Inspector has friends in very high places." There was another pause. "So, in answer to your previous question … I don't know, but I'll be finding out."

By this time, the Inspector had walked up to the patio doors and tapped lightly on the glass. He indicated to the silent man that he wished to have words with him. The silent man rose and went outside; they spoke together for twenty to thirty seconds. The silent man returned and, without entering, opened the patio doors. With one hand on the door handle, he leaned in and said, "Mrs O'Neil, Gill, would it be possible to continue our conversation in perhaps a couple of days?"

I got up off the couch and stepped out into the garden: the day was turning out quite pleasant I said, questioningly, "Yes, I should think so. Has something happened?"

As the Inspector again made a phone call, the silent man replied, "No, nothing serious, just some more information that has come to light, and we need to travel back to London."

His explanation was not very convincing.

The Inspector had finished his call and, coming over to me, said, "I have to apologise for this abrupt departure. It seems we are needed elsewhere. I've called for a car. One should be here directly. In the meantime, may I suggest that one of our technicians visit you, purely as a precautionary measure. But I would like to ensure that your visitor left no eavesdropping devices."

"Why would he leave eavesdropping devices?" I said.

His reply was, "Well, if you've had no contact with this man for such a long period, how can he ascertain the progress you're making with the book? Also he may have pre-empted our visit and might be interested in our progress."

The Inspector noted the look of anxiety on my face and said, "You could employ someone yourself. I can supply you with the details of a number of companies if you are concerned about your private data. The person I would recommend is discreet, reliable and above all honest, and the cost will come out of the police budget. Take a couple of days to think about it and, in the meantime, I'll send you the information."

I think the sudden end to our meeting and the revelation about eavesdropping still resonated; my speech seemed laboured, and I had difficulty comprehending all that was said. I was apprehensive about re-entering the house.

The Inspector, clearly concerned, said, "Mrs O'Neil, It's only a precautionary measure. Don't let it phase you. There's probably nothing to be concerned about. It will just provide you with peace of mind, that's all."

The silent man, who had been overhearing our conversation, said, "Please don't worry. The Inspector here will be in touch in the next few days."

All our eyes were then taken by the appearance of a dark grey car turning into the drive. The Inspector climbed in beside the driver. The silent man began to unwrap yet another sweet as he climbed into the back seat and, just before he pulled the door closed, said, "Loved the hash."

Within a few moments the car was away, and I was left wondering just what I had got myself into.

A New World Order

Annette Phillips

"She's got quite an unusual birthday present for you, Nan…. you will humour her, won't you?"

Nan's daughter Sheila was fussing around, wiping the dishes, checking her cupboards. Things she was more than capable of doing. Suddenly the back door shot open, and her granddaughter tumbled into the kitchen and rushed up to her Nan to give her a big hug. They had a special relationship.

"Oi you! Don't I get one too?"

"Of course. Have you told her yet what we've got her?"

"No, but remember her knees have been playing up, you can't expect too much of her!"

Layla was unperturbed and rooted through her school bag, pulling out an envelope which she pushed into Nan's hand.

"It wasn't easy to get, hope you're going to like it!"

Bemused, Nan opened the envelope and pulled out three tickets. They were for a football match; she didn't do football since Jim died.

"It's special, Nan, it's the women's European Cup semi-final at Bramall Lane. All of my teammates are coming. We'll get you there somehow."

A smile crept into her face as she looked over Layla's head to Sheila who didn't look too happy.

"I'm game for anything, thank you love, what a present."

They didn't have long to get organised as the match was only a few days away. Somehow Sheila commandeered a friend to drop them off close to the Blades ground. Nan hobbled through the turnstile and the crowd on her two sticks and into the stand remembering trips from long ago. It was electric, people eager to get to their seats, but respectful not jostling her, Sheila and Layla either side of her. The stairs were a bit of a challenge, but they were soon in their seats. Looking around she could see all sides were rammed. Full capacity. The Swedish and UK flags were brought out, anthems played. All was a flurry of flags, music, whistles, whole families cheering. A tumble of colours and noise. She was in her element.

"That's the captain Nan, Beth Meade," Layla pointed to a woman warming up energetically. "My namesake,' thought Nan, 'has to bring luck."

She had done a bit of research and found the Lionesses had got to this stage three times before, but a lot of people really rated their new manager, Sarina Weigman, so there was a lot of hope. She felt Layla's hand clasp hers and raise it into the air, the whistle had gone, they were off.

They had good seats at the side only a few rows up. She looked at her daughter who had relaxed for once and was watching animatedly. Freed from the pressures of her demanding job and being a sole parent, lost in the game.

The start was fraught, Sweden had a lot of possession. Then, after half an hour, seemingly from nowhere, Beth Meade scored. Nan found herself on her feet, arms in the air, cheering. After that it only got better. Layla was like a jack-in-the-box, her excitement and joy so visible. As a player, she understood all the moves, fouls, off-sides and kept Nan up to date with a running commentary. She knew all the players and shouted their names as three more goals followed - from Lucy Bronze, Alessio Russo and, in the last minutes, Fran Kirby. The crowd at the end went berserk. The cheering, whistling and flag waving went on and on. Everyone was so energised and happy, more than any of the matches she had come to with Jim. There was no animosity in the air, everyone was hugging, even Swedes with English supporters.

They left the stadium before people started to disperse. Nan could feel her knees going and didn't want to leave it too long, although it took a while to prise Layla away from her school and team- mate Julie.

"Did you see Mary Earp's in goal Julie?" Her friend played that position.

"Sure did, we're going to have to practice some of those moves Layla. I'm just over the moon. Wembley here we come!" They did a dance on the spot with their banners in the air.

Nan met her friend Nancy in the supermarket queue some days later. They had been pals for a very long time, back to early school days. They still only lived a few streets away. After chatting for a while Nancy said, "Have you been watching it, Beth, the women's football? We were right keen, back in the day, weren't we?"

"Too right we were, but it wasn't easy was it."

"We were going somewhere, you and me. You could have made it professionally I reckon."

"Do you think? Except it was banned, Nancy, in the 60s and 70s. The FA Council said football was unsuitable for females and not to be encouraged. Well eat your words!"

"Such a shame, thank God things have moved on, but not without a fight….do you think the women are bringing it home? Something the men haven't done in an awful long time!"

"I hope so. Why not come around to mine, bring Sid if you want to, my daughter and granddaughter Layla will be there. She plays you know; she took me to see the semi at Bramall Lane, it were brilliant Nancy, just brilliant."

So they all met up days later at Nan's flat to watch the final. The women did it. The Lionesses, 'they brought it home'. England 2 Germany 1. Wembley, as was the nation, was overjoyed. The manager, Sarina, before she was hoisted at shoulder height around the pitch, sent a prayer upwards to the heavens. Kissing an amulet to her recently deceased and beloved sister hoping she was watching from the heavens.

A couple of weeks later Layla called at Nan's flat on the way back from school. She found Beth at the kitchen table on her laptop, glasses on the end of her nose peering at the screen, papers scattered beside her and pen in hand.

"What's all this Nan?"

"Thought I might give you a hand, love. You said you didn't know what to do for your school project. What about this…a history of women's football….?"

She paused. "In the 1920s and before the 1st World War, or before your mum or even I were around, women's football was more popular than men's, and played to bigger crowds. It wasn't until after the war that the FA put a ban on women playing using any teams' grounds. That put paid to women playing professionally, or very much at all."

Soon Layla and her grandmother were poring over the information she had gathered, and she began telling Layla her own experiences of playing football, something she had not done before. It was like memories had been unearthed and Nan could see there was a new world order where women's football would grow the world over as it had once before. She hoped she and Layla could celebrate this new world order together and it would give Layla the confidence to be anything she wanted.

New Springs

Penny Wragg

Flo sighed with pleasure. "This bed is so comfortable," she thought. She let her head sink back into the pillow and stretched out her arms, luxuriating in the softness of the mattress which moulded itself around her body. For the first time ever, she had no backache, not a twinge. The smell of the fresh clean sheets reminded her of fields in summer. She opened one eye, fighting against waking up properly. She wanted to lie here forever, next to the man of her dreams. She could feel the familiar shape of him lying next to her, but not encroaching on her space. There was something to be said for a king-size bed, and this new mattress was such an improvement on the old one, no old springs poking out and jabbing you in the ribs as you rolled over! Doug, her husband of nearly fifty years, would surely agree.

Sunlight streamed in through the window. It was even brighter than usual. She knew it was time to open both eyes and sit up to face the day. Yet, something felt odd. She felt slightly disorientated.

◊

On the other side of town, Brian had set his alarm clock for 6.30 am so he wouldn't be late for work. Routine was important to him. First, a wash: a thorough strip wash, not a new-fangled shower, and just a weekly bath on a Sunday. Secondly, get dressed: the same grey work suit and matching tie which he had been wearing every day for years, with a white shirt changed twice a week. Thirdly, breakfast: always porridge, followed by white toast and orange marmalade. He left the house at 7.45 am in time to catch the 8.00 am bus at the end of the high street. He would arrive at work by 8.30 am.

This particular morning, the traffic crawled at a snail's pace because of roadworks, so he reached into his pocket for his favourite science fiction paperback. It wasn't there. Drat! Where had he put it? He felt his bunch of work keys in his left hand jacket pocket. Surely he normally kept them in the right hand one? He had to admit that he was slowing down and becoming a bit forgetful. Something niggled at his brain, something he should have done but hadn't. What was it?

Flo had settled back into a lovely dream about a magic garden. She smiled in her sleep. Doug hadn't stirred. Who knew what he was dreaming about? Probably cakes, as he had rather a sweet tooth. His body shape was proof of that! She was vaguely aware of sounds coming from nearby, and laughter which gradually grew louder. She woke up with a start. Panic seized her as she stared into several smiling faces!

"Doug, Doug, wake up!" she shrieked, for suddenly realisation dawned and memories came flooding back.

His breath was coming in gasps. Blood rushed to his head. His fingers gripped his keys hard, and he couldn't let go. For he knew what he had done, or rather not done. He was bound to get the sack.

It was rather late in the afternoon of the previous day when Flo had at last managed to persuade Doug to come with her to choose a new mattress. She couldn't stand the old one a minute longer. The springs had gone, and she didn't want the spring to go out of their marriage too, not after all their years together and still having a surprisingly good time in bed together every night.

They arrived at a popular store called *Eeze Beds* where they were met by a strange looking hippy type of assistant with long hair and buck teeth. His name label read *Dylan.*

"Hey man," he said, "Would you like me to outline the pros and cons of the different mattresses we have in stock? It's important to choose exactly the right one."

Flo and Doug hadn't known this was going to be so complicated, but Dylan proved to be very helpful. He carefully explained the pros and cons of a foam mattress versus an inner spring one. Tactfully he whispered in Flo's ear when Doug wasn't listening that the inner spring gave more support for the heavier person. Flo giggled. Dylan suggested that the best way forward was to try out a few different mattresses in store. He winked at her and led the way to the king-size bed section.

"Take as much time as you need," he said. "You don't have to decide today. Mull things over at home if you like."

Doug was a little embarrassed, but Flo couldn't wait to get started. However, once he got going, he entered into the spirit of it! After about thirty minutes, Dylan came across to them.

"I've got to finish my shift now as I'm going to the dentist, but I'll leave you in Brian's capable hands. He gestured to an older assistant who was, Flo thought, the epitome of grey. He smiled at them tentatively.

"He may seem a bit slow, man, but he's been here a long time and has a wealth of experiences with mattresses. There's nothing he can't tell you about springs. There's another hour before he is due to lock up."

He winked again at Flo and waved goodbye.

"If you've any questions, don't hesitate to ask me," said Brian in a monotone, and proceeded to leave them to it.

Flo and Doug had tried every mattress in the shop and Flo was leaning towards memory foam. Doug just wanted to get home for his tea. Flo spotted a beautiful bed with a memory foam mattress in the shop window.

"Just one more, Doug" she pleaded. "I've almost decided."

They lay on the mattress and sighed. It was the most comfortable one by far.

"I'm so tired," said Flo. "I'll just shut my eyes for a minute."

Judging by the snores emanating from the other side, Doug had already nodded off.

Brian finished the tidying up and counted the balance from the till. All was quiet. He was looking forward to going home for his tea which would be a Fray Bentos steak pie in a tin, being as it was Thursday. He locked up and went for the bus.

And that was how Flo and Doug woke up in the shop window to see many smiling faces focussed on them. People were standing on the pavement pointing and laughing. Colour flooded Flo's cheeks. At least, she thought, we've still got our clothes on!

"Get up, Doug! We've got to get out of here!"

Doug couldn't move. He was having a panic attack.

At that moment, Brian appeared, waving his keys and apologising profusely, quickly followed by Dylan who was carrying a Costa coffee and eating a raw carrot. He quickly went to find a paper bag for Doug to breathe into. Then a very smart red-haired gentleman approached.

"Good morning, sir, madam. I'm Mr Rusty, the store manager. I can't apologise enough for what's happened. Someone will be getting their cards." He looked pointedly at the trembling Brian.

"No, no," insisted Flo. "There's really no harm done."

They all stood eyeing one another awkwardly.

And that was how Brian was given another chance, but he decided to retire a few months later. He now spends his time building a model railway which was something he'd always wanted to do.

And that was how Flo and Doug acquired a brand-new foam mattress for absolutely nothing, together with a complimentary set of luxury bedding. And every night they look forward more than ever to bedtime and take it in turns to say to each other,

"Time for bed? Say *Eeze Beds!*"

Author's note

With thanks to that iconic television programme *The Magic Roundabout!*

The Mayor, Her Lover, His Wife and the Rat

Glen Fryer

The morning had come and gone, so too had the afternoon, now it was part way through the evening; all was not well in the Town Hall.

The Lady Mayor sniffed with derision and fluttered her hands at the secretary.

"For goodness' sake," Deirdre, "take the files and put them in the storeroom. I need to make a call to the Labour MP about the total mismanagement of that block of apartments the council is offering for a pittance; dear oh dear."

Deirdre turned away and padded out of the room. She was seething. "A whole week of rooting through these damned files, and what for? To be unceremoniously fluttered at and told to be off, then put them all away again."

For several months now, a mumbling had been heard from the conference room. Occasionally a thump on the table as an angry individual emphasised discontent at what was being said. The woman seated at the head of the table could be heard tutting, even if you didn't actually stand outside the door and actively listen.

"Well, I'm dashed if you think you can get away with this. Those homes will be sold over my dead body," she could be heard saying in a purring voice, hoping that softer tones may thwart any imminent belligerence.

A distinct rustling of papers; coffee cups placed with an unnecessary bang on to the saucer; not everyone of course, just those with whom the mayor had an issue. Rosemary Donaldson was feisty, and she'd maintained her role as Mayor for three consecutive years. This lengthy term had given her ideas above her station and several councillors objected to her continued heavy handedness. For some time, they had been trying to sell off a block of flats. The sale would earn the treasury a handsome sum, each apartment being sold for some £145,000. Times twelve, this would make over a million pounds to pay for repairs around the city.

Rosemary was adamant that housing was needed for constituents who had nowhere to live and that rent collected would do much the same, albeit over a longer period.

Bob Morgan, transport officer, was furious. He knew the likelihood of rent being successfully collected was low. He muttered furiously about the stupidity of the mayor. She had no power over their decisions, but everyone was afraid of upsetting her, and he needed that money for the upkeep of his department.

Deep into the night, he tossed and turned in his bed, trying to figure out a way to stop her from ruling the roost. "Good grief, we councillors are a malleable crew,' he thought. 'I'm going to remove this total monster if it's the last thing I do."

He thumped his pillow, then pressed his weary head into the fluffy contents and tried to sleep. By the morning, he'd hatched a plan: he wasn't a man known for violence, nor had he ever really divulged bad thoughts about anyone; but this woman … He seethed as he brushed his teeth, and ground those freshly minted molars whilst chewing his toast and swallowing coffee as if it had bits of shrapnel swimming around.

Rosemary was, as you would imagine, blissfully unaware of the thoughts that were plaguing one of her comrades. She did her usual strutting around, organising her day-to-day life as Mayor. Duties included fund-raising, opening various events and as already seen, interfering with council business. Today, she was having a day in the office. Her secretary, Deirdre, was annoying her intensely; just being Deirdre was enough, and today, she wasn't feeling well. Yesterday's altercation had rattled her immensely, and she decided to take out her spite on her secretarial help. Within minutes, Deirdre was rooting through files in the cupboard down the corridor.

By the end of the afternoon, there were two people suffering with malice aforethought.

It was towards the end of the calendar month, the finance department had closed their doors and pressed ahead with calculations concerning the apartment building which had incensed Rosemary so much. The legal team had set up advertising, announcing the forthcoming sale, and hired an estate agent willing to organise viewings. When Rosemary got wind of this, she had an absolute tantrum, and stormed into the MP's office. Throwing her hands up in the air, she accidentally caught him on the nose.

"Ouch, you total witch!" he yelled, but he managed to restrain himself from punching her in return.

"How dare you continue with this barbaric decision to sell those apartments? Places meant for homeless people here in our city," she screamed, ignoring his obvious distress.

"You are merely the mayor," he yelled back. "I'mb not answerable to you. Geb out ob my officth."

Rosemary stood her ground. "No, you insufferable clown. I cannot turn my back on these poor creatures. How would you like to live in such squalor ...eh?"

The MP stared back at her, "Push off, you cow. We're in the last stages of releasing these dwellings to people who can pay for them, so your comment of 'over my dead body' IS PERFECTLY OKAY BY ME!"

She blanched, turned on her heel, and positively tore down the corridor to her parlour, a handkerchief held to her mouth as she sobbed.

(Can I propose there were now three in the clan who'd had enough?)

Deirdre stared at the distraught woman and suggested a cup of tea.

The mayor glared at her and nodded. With the tea made, Deirdre decided to go. Time had moved on swiftly and she couldn't quite believe it was already nearly eight o'clock in the evening. She didn't get paid for this loyalty, and it was a good job Norman understood her commitment to the smooth running of Rosemary's life. As she moved along the corridor, she went over the contents of the files she was now carrying to the archives. "Nonsense in this day and age," she fumed. "Everything should be on a computer file, not stored in a fusty old room besieged by spiders and whatever else chooses to lurk in the corners." She halted outside the offending cupboard and reached to open the door. A row of filing cabinets stood in a line, each storing decades of council information, deals, sales, purchases, agreements and so on. Deirdre pulled open the drawer marked 'Housing' and started to replace the files. If she had her way, she would compile a complete inventory of what these stupid cabinets contained onto a computer and use this space more productively. Her mind shifted ever so slightly to the possibility of shutting the irritating biddy in it for life …

Rosemary was thorough, too thorough for some. She'd become incensed over the sale of those apartments, and it had made her waspish to the point where Deirdre was wishing something bad would happen and remove her from office. Her journey home was filled with loathing and as she threw open her front door she screeched, "I've had enough of that harridan. Get me a drink!"

Norman dutifully poured out the red wine and emptied crisps into a bowl to share. He made himself a gin and tonic, and prepared to take the flak. He had also resigned himself to making dinner, cleaning the house, going shopping and tending the laundry. All this whilst Deirdre worked diligently for the mayor, coming home later and later. He banked down the slow burn in his chest and hoped one of them would leave and give him a breather. Although he secretly thought Deirdre rather liked wallowing in martyrdom.

One day, a few weeks later, he came home and announced he had joined a drama group. Deirdre wasn't amused, but could do little to stem his desire to act, so busy was she with Rosemary's diary. It didn't however stop her from giving him a piece of her mind. After all, she was his wife and he needed guidance.

"What an utter fool you will make of yourself. You will certainly stutter and spit into the face of your co-actors." She burst into shrill sarcastic laughter and bowed her way from the room.

He sighed. 'Whatever,' he thought.

Norman's life dragged on, and it was one Friday evening as he was en route to the drama group that a chance encounter with Rosemary sparked off a frisson of desire. It was totally unintentional, but when he spotted her waddling down the aisle of ready-meals, he decided to make himself known. He'd never spoken to her; in fact, all he knew about her was what a tyrant she was. He was so intrigued he stopped her and said, "Hello, Lady Mayor. How nice to see you, I'm Deirdre's husband. I don't think we've met?"

Rosemary halted and smiled indulgently at him, her fictitious mayoral hat instantly upon her head.

"Oh," she replied, "how very nice to meet you at last. Deirdre hasn't mentioned you much, and I was beginning to think you were a figment of her imagination." With that she burst into peals of mirth and put her hand fondly upon his arm.

He was caught unawares, and the frisson shot through his sex-starved body. Impulsively he replied, "Can I help take your shopping home? Deirdre is still working, which I assume is to do with an important date?"

"Oh, no, not really. I think your wife likes to think she's indispensable, and yes, what fun. Come home with me and we'll open some wine." Her eyes sparkled, her bosom shaking with her laughter.

Norman was all of a dither. This wasn't at all like the image he'd had of her. Quickly he grabbed the few items he needed and hurried to the checkouts. Outside, he followed her home, which was some four miles away on the west side of the city. The drama class was now completely forgotten and, as he went through the door of Rosemary's home, he felt his blood thicken.

It was several hours later when he emerged. It had certainly been entertaining. His hands were still shaking, his pulse beat against his temple, and he could hardly believe the events which had taken place. It did not leave much to the imagination; consequently, visits to her home became a regular feature. Of course, he showed up at the drama group, but started to slip away an hour earlier in order to give the Lady Mayor all she desired.

Deirdre hadn't a clue about his liaison with her boss, except a somewhat curious difference in the mayor's behaviour.

"Sometimes she seems almost nice," she said as they walked arm in arm around the park. "Maybe she has a lover." She burst into peals of laughter, similar to those with which Rosemary had trapped Norman recently.

He paled and joined in her mirth saying, "Unlikely, from what you've told me. Who would want to bed that?"

Weeks passed until one day Rosemary came up with the inevitable announcement. "Norman, we must go public."

'Christ almighty!' he thought.

Over the course of their affair, he had learned much about her, including her phobia of rats. Now the thought of being exposed had terrified him, and the fear of Deirdre's impending wrath almost finished him off. He, like Bob, was about to hatch a plan, one which would see the mayor off. Her desire to announce their tryst was relentless. He sweated day and night, could hardly eat or sleep and, during the wee small hours, he found himself creating the perfect murder. He planned it to the 'nth degree, found a detailed map of the Town Hall, and examined every possibility of unseen entrances and exits. He would have to wait for the right moment. A visit to a pet shop well away from their area saw him choosing a large and disgusting sewer rat. It was huge - stiff greyish hair, a long whippy tail wagging behind it. Prominent yellow teeth and beady eyes. It was enough to give even the hardiest individual a serious fright. Hidden in his shed, he made it a run, nailing together boxes which ran around the perimeter of his ten-foot by six-foot bolt hole. Deirdre never came near this place, and he felt certain the rat would be a quiet enough creature. He'd discovered the perfect entry into the Town hall and, planning to be armed with a set of tools, he would make his way upstairs undetected disguised as a workman, his 'toolbox' containing his mate, now christened 'Satan'. He figured it would be easy to let his comrade free to do the job of a lifetime and thus save him from the horror of going public. His carnal desire took a nosedive, visits to Rosemary waned, much to her dismay, but she reckoned she had him hook, line and sinker. She could wait, after all, and she had waited for forty years before finding a man. He was probably trying to find a way of confessing to his peevish wife.

It took six months for him to lay out these plans; the timing, every eventuality covered, examined, and rehearsed to the point of sheer exhaustion. He was shattered, and in order to give himself a bit of space he invented a weekend away with his workmates. "A bonding experience," he said smoothly over breakfast. Deirdre was surprised. He'd never previously shown interest in such things, and she started to protest … then suddenly it occurred to her it would be rather nice to have the weekend to herself. She would book some beauty treatments and stroll down the high street where she'd seen a painting she thought would do for the dining room. She would have the picture up on the wall before Norman returned from his stupid bonding. She waved him off and set off in a cheerful mood towards town.

Meanwhile, Norman was wandering along the cliffs of Scarborough, his hands stuffed into his pockets. Oh, the relief to get away from both women! He seriously considered doing a disappearing act, trying to start again. Deirdre was right, her sermon late the night before had left him feeling utterly deflated, the final shot being, "What had he ever achieved?"

"I'll tell you what I've achieved," he snarled. "The stupid mayor and her lust, a wife who couldn't care less, and a fat bleeding rat who may or may not do a good job of frightening Rosemary out of her wits, and out of my life!" He found a pub and dived in, ordered a pint and prayed for an existence without threatening women.

Saturday evening alone was just the antidote to a snivelling husband and a demanding boss. Deirdre opened a bottle of wine and popped her meal into the microwave. "I'll just go and find a

157

picture hook from the shed," she said to herself and off she trotted feeling so serene.

"Oh, what's the rancid smell?" she said as she pushed open the shed door. Norman's domain was usually so tidy, but now, well, what on earth were all these boxes? She advanced and made her way towards the largest of the boxes where, to her utter horror, she came eyeball to eyeball with a big ugly rodent. They stared at one another as she screamed and held her nose. It sat up on its hind legs and held its little hands together as if in a plea to be reprieved from whatever she may be about to do.

She turned and ran, gagging, back to the house. "Wait till he gets back! What's he thinking of? Has he gone round the twist? What a horrible thing that was!"

Sunday evening arrived and Norman, reluctantly, set off back to his home. The weekend away hadn't done much to build up his courage, but at least it had been quiet. The sound of the sea and seagulls were the only noises he'd experienced, and it had been bliss. The driveway loomed, and he drove over the bump and parked next to Deirdre's vehicle. As he opened the door to the house, a blast of vocal abuse came down the hallway like a green ball of smoke. Recoiling against the wall, he waited for the inevitable smack which usually followed.

If you can imagine the worst scene, the most acrimonious and dirt-slinging row, then you have correctly summed up the greeting waiting for Norman after his bogus weekend away. A heavy pall of anger hung over the house, and both parties were exhausted after the unholy row which had ensued. Norman promised to get rid of the rat, wouldn't explain why he had bought it, and sulked.

A week later, he had reached boiling point and decided his plan should go ahead; it would have to be done. He went out to the shed to have a last chat with Satan and opened the door of the cage. The creature had gone; gone! No amount of searching solved the fact that it was absolutely not in his shed.

He suffered waves of panic as he juggled what would be worse, another show-down with Deirdre when Rosemary exposed their affair or the long shot that, if the assassin hadn't done a runner, Satan might've managed to pull off the phobic fatality of the mayor. He decided Rosemary would ruin his life, plus his mother would disown him, for hadn't his father run off with the secretary? He sat and waited for signs that Deirdre knew the rat had legged it. He gave up the acting classes and the liaison with the mayor, telling her he thought Deirdre was suspicious. Rosemary had gone eerily quiet and he wondered what she was planning. *It was* ominous. He worried too that Deirdre might be planning something. And where was the friggin' rat!

Chance. Chance is all you need, and a modicum of luck. And it was this which brought the whole sorry affair to a head. One afternoon, the same week after Norman's bogus bonding, Deirdre overheard her boss chatting to one of her cronies over the phone, amongst the words spoken were 'Norman? Norman?' She listened on and learned, to her total dismay and fury, that her husband had been having his way with the mayor. Oh, the disbelief! And with that rotund hag! She almost choked in her wrath. She kept calm, went home, and watched her husband intently. Nothing untoward, but he was edgy, she could tell. He was so transparent. In fact, why hadn't she clocked it earlier? "Drama classes my arse!"

The day arrived and it took all her courage to empty the rat into her tote bag, zip it up and carry the filthy thing into the office, then hide it behind the filing cabinet and wait for an opportunity to let it go. She'd given the rat several crusts of toast, and a dollop of Marmite to give it extra oomph. The day wore on so slowly, Rosemary had said she would be working into the evening but told Deirdre to go home. She would be OK.

Deirdre wondered why. Was Norman actually going to arrive and throw the wanton hussy on to the carpet? Ugh! However, it had seemed an eternity before she'd walked back towards that dratted cupboard and prepared to let the fat and stiff-coated rodent loose. She would set it free, go home and then nod sadly as she heard on the news that the mayor had died of fright. The bitch!

Oh, the satisfaction of seeing her husband's face when he too saw the news. The sheer delight that she, she of all people, had pulled off the perfect crime. What luck that Norman had purchased the horrible animal in the first place. It was a curious choice and she didn't think for a moment he knew of Rosemary's phobic horror of rodents.

It had gone. No sign of it anywhere. Yet she knew she had secured it, the zip pulled tight. Where was it? Panic flew around her. She was now full of guilt and quite unnerved. She put the files away and, grabbing the empty bag, she went home. By morning, both Deirdre and Norman were in tatters. Neither one spoke about the rat, each so filled with panic, fright, and regret. Norman had disposed of all the boxes, cleaned out the shed and ditched the plan to murder Rosemary.

At nine next morning, Deirdre went about her usual routine and set off for the Town Hall almost beside herself. What if the rat had done its job? What then? Did she still confront Norman? Or would she just let it settle until - *wham*! - sometime in the future, she would let him know. Oh yes, she would let him know ... she knew!

She was still totally unprepared for what greeted her, even with the knowledge of ratty on the loose. A night spent tossing and turning; hoping it would just disappear and let Rosemary off the hook, alas …

There lay the mayor, her arm lying at an awkward angle, her stocking tops on show. Deirdre, without thinking, quickly straightened Rosemary's skirt, decently covering her rather ample thigh, and glanced repulsively at what looked like the lifeless face of her boss. An image

162

of Norman fondly stroking that upper leg flashed through her mind and she felt the urge to kick that fleshy bum.

"Oh my God! My God!" she whispered instead, the full impact sweeping over her, the fear of death welling up into her throat until she almost threw up. Rosemary's eyes were still open in terror, and she stared sightlessly back at the white face of Deirdre.

The security man would be on duty, taking over from the night watchman; he arrived at seven in the morning to take up his long and boring partnership with the cameras, so she charged out and down the staircase towards the office where Stanley Biggin would be at his desk. The room stank of tobacco smoke. She pursed her lips in irritation; smoking was not allowed. Stanley was leaning back in his swivel chair, head up as he savoured the smoke rings emitted from his mouth, completely oblivious to her arrival.

"Stanley!" she shouted. He almost tipped over backward, then hastily put out his cigarette and felt the blood rush to his face with the embarrassment of being caught.

"Deirdre, tha' looks right mad. What's up?"

163

"What's up? I'll tell you what's up, Rosemary looks as if she's dead. She's lying on the carpet in a most undignified position and I want to know why you didn't spot an intruder."

Stanley gawped at her, she looked deranged, her spectacles fallen askew. He paled. Oh how he paled. But he stood up.

"I'd better phone the police then, eh?"

"Eh? I would say it's worth more than an 'eh'," Deirdre snapped. She grabbed the phone out of his hand and dialled 999.

A quite nicely spoken voice answered, "Emergency, which service do you require?"

"Policssse," Deirdre replied, the emphasis on the final 's' in order to clarify the gravity of her request. She took a deep breath and hurriedly explained the need for police assistance.

It took all of five minutes for a squad of plain-clothes men to arrive, all looking severely self-important. Detective Dixon stroked his thin pointed chin as he surveyed the mayor.

"Tut, tut, what a carry on. Poor Rosemary. Who on earth would want to do her in?"

Deirdre sucked in her breath. "Well obviously someone who didn't like her." Having straightened her glasses, she now realised they were steaming up. She pushed them further up the bridge of her nose and fumbled demonstratively for her tissues.

She explained the incident as best she could, telling the detective how she had left the mayor here in the parlour the previous evening, perfectly fit and well, then the discovery this morning of her lying on the Persian carpet adorning the solid wood floor of her parlour. She upped the concern for her beloved boss, adding, 'Poor Rosemary, yes, we all know she's quite a tartar but to be murdered, well that's going a bit too far in my opinion. I left her here, as I said, 'Yes, she's had several run-ins with our MP and Bob from transport, but surely, no one would actually murder her. Oh dear, what a shock to find the Lady Mayor this morning in a decidedly uncomfortable position on the rug. So help me God.'

She watched, fascinated, as the serious face of the detective scribbled his notes into a small black notebook.

"I've had a word with our security man," she continued. "He said he saw no one entering the building. There's a camera on each floor, so he either left the room just at the wrong moment, or he was dozing. His is not the most scintillating occupation in the world I know, but he gets a good salary. He'll be held to account for his unprofessional approach to his job."

Deirdre stopped nattering and looked at the detective with wide eyes. "Good grief," she thought. "How prissy of me, I sound just like Rosemary. Stanley needs this job, he has mouths to feed."

The detective nodded silently as he continued to write notes. "Horrible, this is," he muttered, then glanced out of the window adding, "I've sent for an ambulance and we should hear the sound of …"

With that a loud noise announced its imminent arrival, growing louder as it roared up the precinct and ground to a halt outside the Town Hall. A collection of various individuals had gathered by the Town Hall steps, among them the assailant, eager to watch the drama, watching with a collection of innocent bystanders, including ragged vagrants, street entertainers and those heavily laden with cheap fruit and veg from the market. Two men dressed in green jumped from the ambulance and tore up the steps into the foyer, a stretcher held between them. Bob had just joined this crowd of individuals, having heard of the disaster which had left the mayor dead and it crossed his mind that it looked like a comedy show. He could almost see Little and Large, yes, they were a bit like them, one thin and wiry while the other puffed his cheeks out as they raced up the steps and disappeared. It was only moments later when three white-coated individuals arrived in a police car and bustled towards the scene with a little more intent than the ambulance crew who were just happy to remove the body and drive her to the mortuary until her case had been investigated. Bob nodded in satisfaction; job done.

Upstairs cameras clicked, and one of the forensic team drew a line of chalk around the form of the mayor, making Deirdre wince,

"Oh, this will ruin the carpet, and we haven't got the budget for cleaning it." She stood twitching her fingers around her ruined tissues and looked for any signs of a disturbance: it was vital. Nothing looked out of the ordinary. The whisky bottle had been knocked over, Rosemary's glasses were still sitting imperiously on the desk and, except for a couple of shuffled papers and an empty cocoa mug, it looked pretty much as it always did. She hadn't thought Rosemary was a drinker, and to see this bottle half-empty surprised her. People continually surprised one; for all she knew, Rosemary could have fallen in a drunken state and caused her own demise.

When the three forensics had finished, Rosemary was lowered onto a stretcher and carted off by the two men. For what it was worth, they didn't seem eager to use the newly installed lift, an easier job than carrying the hefty figure of Rosemary down the stairs. But down the stairs they went, the size difference worked here because the angle of the steps balanced them out. 'Large,' puffing less, with sweat beaded along his fleshy forehead, going first, closely followed, (a stretcher's length behind) by 'Little,' whose biceps bulged through the green t-shirt, showing a strength quite unexpected considering his little body and shorter legs. As they gallantly proceeded out of the door, the crowd 'oohed' and 'aahed' their commiseration for the demise of the local celebrity. Rosemary Donaldson, Lady Mayor, had been feared as much as she was loved … well not loved: nobody could confess to loving her. She was an absolute cow at the best of times, but sadly, in a trice, they were murmuring compliments about how diligently she had worked and how she would ultimately be hard to replace.

The assailant sloped off.

For several weeks, the Lady Mayor, loved or loathed, lay in a mortuary as the police endeavoured to flush out a murderer.

A careful search of the parlour uncovered very little. Prints taken from Rosemary's cocoa cup and whisky tumbler, along with prints from the edge of the desk, her diary, her spectacles case and anything else she or, more critically, the perpetrator of this dreadful crime may have handled. The one curious discovery was a trail of droppings, too large to be mice, more likely to be that of a rat. This was exceedingly odd: the place was the domain of Roger the Dodger, resident fat cat, whose title alluded to the fact he would not be handled; picking up was a no-no and he ruled the entire Town Hall. Many of the employees had sported inflamed scratches, and sometimes, left to pick up his excrement. He cared not a jot for anyone save himself, and it was highly unlikely anything in the rodent family would survive a week into setting up a home in his domain. No; rat droppings were a very unusual discovery. The detectives ruminated about this over a pint in the local area as they discussed the poor list of findings.

"Very queer, I say," Detective Dixon muttered, the pint of stout ale sliding down very nicely after another day's fruitless search. "Why were there what looked like rat droppings in that room? I mean the cat is notorious for its mouse hunting. Seems odd, as if a rat was deliberately brought in deliberately."

His team looked blankly at him. There weren't many people to ask about Rosemary's personal life, very few to outline her likes, dislikes, fears, interests; you know, usual stuff. It seemed Rosemary Donaldson was a loner. She lived a comfortable existence in some splendour on the west side of the city; no cats, dogs, budgies nor anything else to crowd her space. She had lived and breathed … and sadly died for the Town Hall, and for her role as Lady Mayor of the city. There wasn't, as far as anyone knew, even any love interest: that, to some, was understandable. She was formidable at the best of times, and trying to conjure up a softer, more amorous side to her nature was difficult. A thorough search within her private residence, the garden and garage had produced nothing. Her diary showed only appointments, save for the mysterious letter 'N' which cropped up at least one day in every month. It could have stood for anything, may have indicated an appointment for any number of reasons. Forensics commented that this initial could stand for Nevoid, properly initialled NBCCS, or Nevoid basal cell carcinoma syndrome.

"Just a thought," one of them commented.

The surgery where she was a patient was called upon to help solve the mystery, but they declared she suffered from nothing debilitating, and was indeed quite a hearty, healthy woman whose face they seldom saw *('Thank goodness.')* for she sometimes swept in unannounced and demanded a health check expecting the doctors to drop everything and attend to her request immediately.

Detective Dixon was building quite a revealing picture of 'poor Rosemary' as he had originally called her, and he was beginning to understand she could have had, after all, a set of rattled individuals who would gladly end her rule in the mayoral parlour. Female detectives searched through her clothing, handbags, jewellery, even her underwear drawer: you never knew. But even that was filled with sensible knickers and sturdy brassieres. It caused a flow of unsuppressed giggling when a young officer found a suspender belt made of black lace with red suspender buttons dangling quite tantalisingly, suggesting a fruitier side to the mayor's past. It had to be the past because no way would it have now fitted around the robust girth of the deceased.

Of course, life must go on, and the employees, frightened they may be the next victim, came armed with various tools of defence. Stanley polished his glasses and actually wore them from now on, as he wiped the nicotine from the security screens and had even polished his shoes. He'd had them re-heeled and they were, if you like, ready for action, mainly an escape if necessary. The MP, James Corton found the absence of Rosemary a secret relief. Gone were the endless phone calls as she harangued him over those bloody flats and he felt all sorts of guilt as he nodded his commiserations about her death, then internally hugged himself with glee that she was out of his hair at last. The endless nattering down his ear had been replaced by such sweet silence he almost wished he knew who had done her in so he could award that person freedom of the city.

"Christ," he thought, "she was only the mayor." Okay, her list of fund-raising activities had always been highly successful, but he reckoned it was more fear than fondness that had actuated it. He leaned back in his chair and put his hands behind his head, "Aah, good riddance to her and her interfering." He picked up the phone and contacted Bob. It was almost too good to be true, and they did their best not to whoop with joy.

Up on the first floor, the Persian carpet was shampooed, and all the furniture thoroughly cleaned and polished after the forensics had finished their task, they basked as the sunshine shone through the long, beautiful window and poured all over the figure of Deirdre. She, after a week's absence due to the 'post-traumatic effects of finding her boss dead', had returned and continued to work. She sat behind Rosemary's desk and dealt with the pile of correspondence that arrived each day, occasionally peering out of the window to admire the fountains in the garden below.

The power suited her. She felt agreeably content as she set up a program on her computer and entered all the information she could lay her hands on. "Really, it was a far more efficient system than the archaic approach the last Mayor had conducted," she thought and smiled with satisfaction, pushing back a recurring niggle concerning Rosemary's accident.

In her role of personal assistant to Rosemary, secretary, according to the vicious tongue of her former boss, she had of course known every little detail of mayoral life. Appointments, including group visits, like the poor children admitted to the stately parlour for a patronising speech from Rosemary, drilling them with the effort one needed to make in order to achieve in life, followed by jammy dodgers and milk. Oh, yes, she knew it all. Often she stayed late after Rosemary herself had gone, attempting to make sure every detail of her day's work was faultless. She knew Rosemary was unmarried, had never been in a long-term partnership, and had been totally dedicated to her ambition of Lady Mayor, and had succeeded in re-election for the past three terms of office, much to the amazement of everyone who knew her, but then, one considered, who could be bothered to try and follow in her very capable footsteps?

There was really only one person who wanted it: Deirdre. She had fervently digested all the requirements needed for the job, noted down everything of importance and, as mentioned, often stayed late, leaving her husband twiddling his thumbs at home.

Now, even without the title, she had launched herself as a desirable candidate for the vacant position. Telephone calls to the councillors went smoothly, she felt her interaction with the MP for their constituency was healthy, her voice did not sound authoritative, she smiled as she delivered information and drank her coffee from Rosemary's old china cup and saucer.

'*Senseless death of Mayor*' headed the front page of the local rag. It went on to describe the life and death of Rosemary, her contribution to the city which had been of such great value to the many citizens living here in this great northern place, then a sad and very short paragraph describing her private life, her home and interests, and activities. The cause of death was, astonishingly, a heart attack, sudden and with no apparent cause. She'd been in good health, if a little overweight, but that would be the result of the plethora of dinners she had attended of late. The police were still investigating the case and hinted that a peculiar set of fingerprints had been found, but not giving anything away about the rat droppings. Several members of the council had offered their assistance, given interviews and generally shown horror that the poor woman had been deprived of any more life. Bob smiled tersely with crossed fingers and had a round of drinks with the MP to silently celebrate her demise … nothing said of course: no need.

Those who did not know her other than from her various mayoral appearances; those seemingly eager women who listened to her as they tried to make their own lives a bit easier, knew nothing of her constant nagging when she was interfering with council activity. They read with sadness of her sudden demise, and wondered who on earth would be able to replace such a worthy individual.

The Mayor's Parlour displayed comfortable lounge chairs and a large highly polished desk which stood in the light that streamed through the leaded windows. Chandeliers hung from the ornately decorated ceiling and lit up the various parts of the room. Besides the desk, a more informal area of settees and chairs graced the patterned carpet, grouped around the oversized and ornately decorated fireplace in that room on the first floor of the Town Hall. A fairly substantial mahogany table, round and highly polished, stood in another part of the room with chairs perfectly placed awaiting those privileged enough to be invited for conferences, open days and once, for the heated debate at which she had drawn in the unwitting MP for. The Victorian building, resplendent with marble flooring and a sweeping staircase, just called one in to enjoy one's working hours. It was indeed a wonderful environment.

Deirdre's sick leave after the discovery of her lifeless boss had Norman going to work earlier and staying out a fraction later to save himself a moment or two of her constant drivel. When, to everyone's surprise, she recovered within the week and returned to her position as personal assistant to the deceased mayor's workload, he nearly found himself paying a trip to the local church to thank the Lord for her quick recovery. Everyone gave her a fond welcome when she reappeared, which she absolutely lapped up. Treading prettily up the steps which would lead her to that fateful room where Rosemary had met her maker, she armed herself with the knowledge that work must go on, especially now Rosemary had gone. She stood in the open doorway and glanced with satisfaction at the beautiful room. The room had been tended carefully by the cleaners, all traces of that dreadful evening obliterated, and now she would spend her days there, completing unfinished tasks. It was, as all good personal assistants knew, their duty to carry on when all was against them.

So began a period of calm. Deirdre went over all the affairs of her previous employer, sorting out the charity days, the fund-raising, the personal appearances and the to-do lists which the mayor had left behind.

Norman breathed a huge sigh of relief: it seemed as though he had had his wish granted, without having had to do his worst. He didn't mention Satan. His clean-up of the shed had gone perfectly. He set fire to the set of plans showing the layout of the Town Hall, and he patted himself on the back. He would be needed to aid the new Mayor as she performed her duties for the city.

This is where we go back to the night Rosemary Donaldson, mayor-elect, lay dead on the floor, eyes wide with terror and rat droppings scattered around her. This is where Detective Dixon had stood puzzled, not knowing why there would be rat poop in the mayoral parlour. Her sudden death, a heart attack, suggested she had been terrified, and the droppings suggested it may be to do with a rodent. But who? Who, apart from her loyal secretary and the cleaners, had had access to the mayor's suite when she was not in the office? And who would want her dead? It was all very peculiar.

Dixon thought about the mayor and her death for months on end. Another thorough search of her home was undertaken. A set of men's toiletries were discovered at the back of a deep cupboard, and a little note attached. He scratched his head as he looked at the name. Mm; curious: everyone had assumed she did not entertain men but here was the evidence, and the note containing a name. But who was he? Did anyone know him? Was he local? And why had he been a secret?

Another six months passed by, and Dixon kept up his search, he trawled through all the entries in the telephone directory, beginning with an 'N' either first or second name. Oh, there were plenty but, after a house-to-house call, it became apparent that none knew anything about her, especially not intimately. Or did they?

He set up a watch, briefed his team about his thoughts, giving them a little inside information concerning the name on the toiletries, and the possibility of who their next suspect might be.

Life in the marital home of Deirdre and Norman went about its muted and distant way. Deirdre kept her mouth closed about the knowledge that her weak and despicable husband had been fornicating with the mayor. She just watched as he slowly withered into a heap of nervous tension. No one mentioned the rat. She certainly didn't: not one word did she let escape from her angry acid mouth. 'Let him sweat' she crowed, Oh she knew, and she would wait until the perfect moment to tell him she had been aware of his infidelity. But who had let the rat out? Or was it just a chance that it had escaped and been the killer without any help from another human being?

A year went by and life settled into the mundane. Deirdre offered herself up as a contender for the Lady Mayor's role: it seemed fitting, and she knew Norman would do his duty, stand beside her, offer her all his support; because he just didn't know how much she knew. It tore him to pieces as he meekly did his best to keep her life running as smoothly as possible. He regretted ever having entertained Rosemary and her lustiness. He regretted ever having thought he was clever enough to actually murder her. The look in Deirdre's eyes told him she was on a mission. The day when she was declared the new Lady Mayor and set about using her talents to raise funds and whatever else she could do to keep her in the public eye, he knew without a doubt that he would be her slave now instead.

Dixon watched as she posed on the Town Hall steps and waved regally to her public.

A picture sailed into his head and a light bulb went off. He saw clearly the assailant, watched the mingling with the small crowd of locals when Rosemary had been carted off to the mortuary.

"The rat!"

It took several months for Dixon to unravel the mystery. He tracked down umpteen pet shops where rats were kept for resale. He could understand a white rat, sleek white hair, pink twitchy nose, and blue beady eyes, quite appealing if you liked rodents, but that one, stiff and grey, pink tail like a slow worm wiggling behind its repulsive body, had not an endearing thing about it. Who would want to own such a creature? Was it deliberately set loose, or had it accidentally found a way in, and conveniently seen Rosemary off? How many people had known she had a phobia? It all seemed to connect.

He sent his officers out to interview all local pet shop owners, until bingo! One day an excited young constable reported he'd found a pet shop on the north side of the city, a shop that sold the ugliest creatures on earth.

'Giant snails, stick insects, reptiles, ugh, and yes brown/grey rats, the sort that caused the great plague!'

Dixon listened carefully and then asked if the shop owner had kept a list of purchasers.

'Yes' came the triumphant reply. 'He had a till roll, the card number on it and the date, time, everything.' The eyes of the constable shone like a kid at Christmas and Dixon clapped him on the back.

"Who?" he asked.

"Norman Dingle," he replied.

A buzz reverberated around the room. Detectives, police constables, forensics and the Chief Super all waiting for the new information Dixon had. The young officer who had unearthed the name of their first suspect was brimming with pride. He'd been in the force for two months and it was his first successful contribution towards solving a crime. Dixon tapped a stick against the whiteboard, where pictures of Norman, of Rosemary, and an image of a sewer rat looked incongruous, like a trio of Neapolitan ice cream colours. Rosemary's face stared out at the congregation, flushed strawberry pink and wide-eyed. Norman, pale and clammy in a cream t-shirt; definitely the 'vanilla' of the piece. Then the rat, hardly chocolate but near enough to imagine it licking its lips after tasting the dregs of cocoa from Rosemary's cup.

"If …," Dixon began to explain, "If this rat was set loose by Norman Dingle, then he is definitely the indirect cause of Rosemary Donaldson's death. I cannot think how it would have found its own way to the Town Hall. I mean, rats are notoriously intuitive, but to hop on a bus and travel incognito to her parlour is preposterous. I think someone, and probably Norman, sneaked the thing in and set it to cause as much damage as it could, namely Rosemary's heart attack and subsequent demise - a nasty thing to happen, whatever your reputation. And," he added, "the information regarding his toiletries found by our detectives, suggests they were a gift from Rosemary, gives him a motive, especially if he was afraid she would expose their relationship. His poor wife, Deirdre Dingle, will be devastated to learn of their liaison, especially as she had worked so hard to keep Rosemary's mayoral duties in tip-top order."

He paused and waited for a reaction from the grouped force. A female officer, clutching a coffee piped up. "Do you suppose his wife found out? And if she did, was it before or after Rosemary's unfortunate confrontation with Mr. Ratty?"

"Good point," he responded. "See what you can discover, snoop around the personal effects kept in our new mayor's desk. She may have kept a diary of events. Though I cannot imagine anyone being so stupid, you never know. 'The female of the species is more deadly than the male.'"

A snigger went round the room. Deirdre's position as mayor had been successful at first, but lately she had begun to interfere with the police, suggesting they do more 'on the beat work' in order to maintain a law-abiding community and it didn't suit them. No one wanted to plod the streets of neighbourhoods looking for rascals, tramps, and drug dealers. It was far cosier to drift around in a squad car, calling into Costa for a coffee or McDonalds for a McFlurry ice cream. Each of them would like to find some dirt to dish concerning her behaviour but, up to now, she was so squeaky clean they felt as though she could not put one foot wrong.

However, a young constable who'd been made to feel like a fool when she publicly chided him wanted nothing more than to expose her as the real culprit. Little did he know he had just solved the whole enquiry.

A routine check of Donald and Deirdre's home brought nothing to the fore. Even so, Donald was held for questioning and detained at His Majesty's pleasure awaiting trial. Deirdre was ashamed, so ashamed of him. How could he put her under the spotlight? Oh, she hated him and his grubby fondling of the deceased mayor's ample bosom. And worse! Oh, how she wanted to rid herself of him altogether, the swine. She visited her solicitor and set about divorcing him. The little runt could rot in hell for all she cared, and she set about clearing out all his things from her home. Whilst she was at it, she started a clear-out for herself by throwing out various items of unused clutter. Several handbags went out, along with inappropriate-heeled shoes, skimpy jumpers and sexy underwear.

"When had she ever worn it anyway? Norman was a cold fish …"

She dumped them at a local charity shop and declared, in her superior voice, that 'A tidy home is a tidy mind.'

Our young and recently embarrassed constable happened to be in that charity shop … you see, it's all chance, and good luck. He watched as she flounced out, then going to the volunteer he asked,

"Hi, I'm a police officer. Please may I search the contents of these bags, the ones just deposited by the mayor? It may help with our inquiries into the death of Rosemary Donaldson, the recently deceased lady mayor of our city."

The volunteer nodded. "Ooh how exciting. Of course," and she handed them over lock, stock, and barrel.

Almost falling over in his haste to deliver the bags, the young man beat it back to the station. He made a quick entry in the register announcing the arrival of evidence, then ran up the stairs until he burst into the incident room and fairly threw the bags at the Detective. Dixon looked up in surprise at the flushed face of his officer and asked what on Earth he was up to.

"I've just spotted our conceited mayor dumping stuff at a charity shop and it occurred to me she might be throwing evidence away, either unwittingly or otherwise. I brought it straight here." With that he emptied the contents over the desk, burying Dixon's hardly finished ham sandwich and tipping his cold coffee over the floor.

"For God's sake," Dixon roared irritably, "look what you've done!"

The youngster blushed but undeterred began to read the list of items in his notebook:

Contents of stuffed bags supplied to a charity shop at 11 am on 16th June 2023 by Mrs Deirdre Dingle, lady mayor of our city.

1, various items of underwear, to include three pairs of lacy stockings.

187

2, a box of jewellery, items of little value; - one necklace with turquoise stones, a silver gilt ring, no stones; a bracelet, made of stone, which could be quartz.

3, handbags of various sizes and colours

3a, cream clutch bag, empty except for a lace handkerchief.

3b, navy shoulder bag containing a photograph of our lady mayor on holiday in Filey eating ice cream,

3c, a large maroon tote, broken zip, containing currants, looks like the remains of a currant bun, possibly a tea-cake.

He looked up, his face slightly deflated.

"Sorry sir looks like I goofed it up."

Dixon shook his head and declared, "You tried. Commendable in the first instance, but let's have another look. Shake out the contents of that large bag."

The constable did as instructed, and Dixon picked up a magnifying glass to see better what these 'currants' were. He looked up, a smile widening across his long sallow face. "By Jove, they're rodent droppings. That rat was in this bag. And who does the bag belong to, eh? Deirdre

Dingle: no other!" He clapped the officer on his back and shook his clammy hand. "Well done lad, well done. You'll be joining the detective squad sooner than you thought!"

It was the sensation of the decade - court case like no other the city had ever experienced. Not one but two people were sent down for the collaborative murder of Rosemary Donaldson, three times elected mayor and undeserving victim of two sinister people. It was in all the news, local and national, a detailed description of the whole sordid operation. A clear and embarrassing account of Norman's lust, and then fear of his affair becoming public. Deirdre's intervention and subsequent removal of the murder weapon … aka Rat-face. The rat, obviously innocent on all accounts, has been trapped not once but twice by the perpetrators involved, and had independently sought revenge on the unsuspecting victim. Rat, by the way, was found in a crumpled heap on the outside back steps, his demise probably that of an interaction with Roger the Dodger, whose reputation still stands to this day.

So let us sum up. Here is the conclusion and the inevitable incarceration of Mr. and Mrs. Dingle.

Murder; premeditated, albeit carried out by the rat whose presence that fateful evening caused the heart of Rosemary to stop when the fat and grisly rodent jumped on to her desk, frightening her to death. His only desire had been to eat what looked like the usual toast and Marmite crust he had lived on for several months. It was assumed she'd screamed and set off for the parlour door, only to trip and fall. The shock was enough to finish her off from what had been a life-long phobia.

Neither Norman nor Deirdre had committed the assault first hand, but it was enough to commit them both for a term in prison.

The judge's voice, nasal and distorted with disgust as he delivered a sentence of five years for being an accessory to Rosemary Donaldson's death, for having supplied the means by which to frighten her and possibly cause her demise. Norman had however not actually taken the animal into the building and so was cleared of any wrong-doing. The fact that he had plotted a way to cause the deceased's health was in itself a crime. He would be sent to an open prison. Community hours would be enforced after his release and his name would be added to a list of offenders for the rest of his life. Norman's head hung in shame. Five years, oh god! But, if he was lucky, it would be over in two and a half. He was led away.

Deirdre Dingle stood in the dock, white-faced, smartly dressed, deliberately still adorned with her mayoral chains, and clutching a bible as if that would get her off lightly.

The Judge took a mouthful of water. He was tired of it all. How on earth did one try to build a worthwhile society of decent citizens when even the mayor was corrupt? The jury had been out and returned with a guilty verdict. That she had taken the rat to the office with the intention of frightening Rosemary out of her wits, an act which had in fact seen the deceased off permanently, was a criminal act. That she had not in fact actually let the beast go had been an accident but, nevertheless, a crime with intent to harm an innocent member of the population had been committed.

"Deirdre Dingle, I sentence you to fifteen years. You will be sent to Durham."

Deirdre sobbed. "Durham, oh the degradation." It wasn't fair; it was Norman who had conjured up and planned Rosemary's murder. He would be swanning about in an open prison, dressed in civvies, while the mayor of the city would languish, in scratchy prison garb; be subjected to all sorts of weird and unhealthy approaches.

Be sure you are aware that pride comes before a fall. She remembered her father delivering these words when she was a child with ambitions.

The door clanged behind her, a room no larger than that dreadful cupboard housing the files at the Town Hall closed around her, a small narrow bed, one sheet, one pillow, one blanket and a sink, no plug, a toilet, no seat was all she had.

On the top bunk, grinning a toothless grin, sat her new room-mate.

"Ello duck. Pleased to meetcha. Got any fags?"

Deirdre groaned.

Seven years later....

There was a rumour that prisoner A143BC was being released. The others were all agog. Wasn't she the rat killer and then the mayor of the city, an upstanding member of the community, pledged to work for and with the public, fund-raising and aiding the lives of those who were deprived?

She had kept her head down and become quite a likeable member of the landing. Written a handbook depicting life as a category B prisoner during the long, lonely hours in a cell, with just your roommate, who could, incidentally, be anyone and not necessarily someone who would stimulate your senses. She had taught Bella Wiggins, her roommate to read, and write.

Deirdre was released one fine spring day, to be greeted by Norman.

"I guess we should call it quits," he said and helped her into the car.

How Is It?

Ken Hutton

Tell it like it is, please, just tell it like it is,
Don't give us speculation or random analysis.
Tell us about the climate stuff and what it really
means,
Is there a point in planting my patch of runner
beans?
Will there be a forest fire or maybe even a flood?
The cows in the field don't seem to care, they just
stand there chewing the cud.
Tell us like it is please, right across the nation,
Will my pot be worthless because of high
inflation?
Tell us about the lost and lonely, and why so
many are poor.
Where has all the money gone? Something's not
right for sure.
Tell us what the prospects are if we get poorly or
sick.
Is there a chance of seeing a doctor really, really
quick?
Tell us what the odds are on the start of World
War Three.

With all the carnage across the world, how
   frightened should we be?
On second thoughts, I've changed my mind, don't
   tell it like it is.

Just give us a bunch of questions for next week's
   bar room quiz.

Filling the Gaps in the History Books

Bob Mynors

History books never tell – can never tell - the whole story. Food sometimes warrants a mention - the infamous restaurant menu from 25th December 1870, whilst Paris was besieged by Prussian forces, which boasted stuffed head of donkey as hors d'oeuvre, consommé of elephant as potage, bear ribs as an entrée and, amongst the roasts, cat flanked by rats. Most characters in history never seem to eat though. Toilet habits get less coverage. George II, Judy Garland and Elvis Presley feature on Wikipedia's **List of People who Died on the Toilet,** *whilst some interesting ways of abluting after defecating may be found at* https://survivalschool.us/top-10-things-wipe-ass-woods/, *but you will never find out if Shakespeare or Bismarck or Sitting Bull ever used them. In this story, however, an attempt is made to throw light on a very different tale that has become accepted history*

Dinner at Lady Stannington's was followed, always, by cards, games played for money, which was often exciting, but the way the hostess arranged the seating could be idiosyncratic. One particular evening, the Lady Veronica was dismayed when, after taking her seat, she saw that oaf Johnny Montagu come and sit on her right. A moment later, his father, the fourth Earl, sat on her left. She and Johnny exchanged some polite conversation, but he was a far-from-entertaining collocutor. He then introduced his father, adding, "Pops used to be First Lord of the Admiralty, you know." The Lady Veronica did know. Johnny tried to continue. "And now he's … erm … what are you now, father?"

"I am Secretary of State for the Northern Department. You should know that: you've been told often enough. If you are going to inherit the title one day, you should pay more attention to affairs of state."

Johnny gulped, then grinned and made his eyes almost pop out of his head. The Lady Veronica, trying to avert this potentially embarrassing situation, said, "Well – I confess I find it a very great honour to find myself between the current Earl of Sandwich and the future one. One might say I have been *sandwiched*."

At this, both men laughed in a very haughty way. Then Johnny said, "I say, that's a jolly clever thing, isn't it, Pops? What?" The fourth Earl looked at his son with disdain. But the son continued. "And I say – I have just had a rather splendid idea. You could use it as the name for that beef and bread thing you always call for where you're at the gaming tables."

The fourth Earl's gaze, still trained on his son, grew harder. The Lady Veronica made her excuses and left

Freddie Fox's Ordeal

Sue Allott

Christmas was over and all were asleep.
Even out in the barn, there wasn't a peep.
Poor Croaky the Cockerel had nodded off too,
So, no-one heard the scritch-scratching
Which seemed to come through
The bottom of the barn door where
Freddie Fox tried digging a hole in the floor,
Hoping to catch a New Year dinner, so
With saliva thoughts flowing, "I'm onto a winner."
He scratched and he dug, paws shaking with glee,
Not giving a thought to his strategy
For catching a fine hen. Oh yes, he could jump,
But what if they weren't in there? He would get the
   hump.

*Then he smelled them; raising an evil smile, he
   began to sing*
How clever I am with this whole dinner thing.
I'm hungry, I'm starving, but nevertheless
*On the other side of this door there'll be one hen
   less!!*

**The front row of hens in the back of the barn
began to rustle. Something was attacking their
sleep pattern. Small throaty sounds were
emitting from the Warrens, then it was carried
on by the Lavenders, the Norfolk Grays, of
which there were only two, which were actually
black in colour, and were also picking up on the
activity. There were a couple of long-legged
Hamburgs, swift hens they were, when occasion
demanded. Then there was Farmer Bob's prize
Sussex pair and his Light Sussex girls. He'd
created a handsome group of rare breeds and
was proud of them, especially their beautiful
free-range eggs.**

It was time to act. The girls were clucking to
each other. Wendy Warren whispered to her row,
"Pass the message on, something's wrong."

Lucy Lavender carried the news to the others.
Gradually all were awake, and they realised Croaky

was still asleep. Susie Sussex was nearest to him, but Henrietta Hamburg beat her to it. With her long legs, she leapt up the haystacks to where he was snoozing, nearly knocking him off his perch with her wings, her beak pecking at his neck.

"What the devil? What's the matter with you? Don't you know it's the middle of the night? What on earth's wrong with you, gal? What a way to behave, Henrietta, I thought I'd taught you better than that. You'll be at the end of the egg-line tomorrow. Ha, I shall give you a miss." He coughed and spluttered trying to regain his balance and composure. He never did like being caught out in the one leg sleeping position whilst in charge.

"Oh, get over yourself Croaky. Wake up. This is an emergency. Something's wrong."

"Wrong? Wrong? What d'ya mean gal, wrong? What could possibly be wrong? We're as safe as houses in here, and don't you forget who's in charge. Go back to your bail, get back to sleep and let me get back to mine." He huffed, and puffed out his chest with irritation, his comb quickly rising, as it did when he was perturbed. "These girls! Always said they were dim," he murmured, ruffling his feathers and gently closing his eyes.

By this time, Henrietta was joined by the others, making sure Croaky didn't fall asleep again, whilst reiterating their fears and thoughts. By this time, Croaky was well and truly awake. He'd no choice but to listen to them.

"If you think you are good at being in charge, then I suggest you get down here to the floor and listen to what we can hear," squawked Nelly, the Norfolk Gray. She shone in the light, her black feathers a rainbow amongst the browns. This was the reason she won her first prize in last year's local farmers' country show, and of this, she was *very* proud.

"Oh alright," sighed Croaky. "Really and truly, this is all too much." He clambered down the bales and fluttered clumsily to the floor. "Now what's this all about girls, eh?"

Lucy Lavender, held up her wings and demanded quiet. "Listen, what's that noise?" She held her breath. Suddenly the sounds of digging and singing became apparent. Although they were at the back of the large barn, sound travelled. The hens were used to waking up to sounds. Usually it was wind or owls landing on the roof. Frightened gasps could be heard from everyone, including

Croaky who realised, with a lot of irritation, that his girls were right to wake him up; after all, he was in charge, and this was an emergency.

"Well, what are we going to do?" He cocked his head on one side, everyone was demanding answers from him.

"Hmm," he croaked quietly. "Well, I have a feeling that this is Freddie's work. I'd recognise that singing anywhere. He's obviously trying to dig underneath the door to get in and do his worst."

Beaks opened, heavily drawn breaths could be detected and chattering commenced.

"No, no - you must stay quiet. Don't want him to know that we're awake and know he's there," commanded Croaky. "Look here, we've got to have a plan, some form of strategy. So, stop your clucking and think!" His beady eyes blinked wildly, and his comb once more began to stand to attention.

"Oh dear, oh dear, oh dear," croaked Lulu Light Sussex. She was the sensitive one and never liked confrontations. "Oh dear, I don't like this at all, oh dear, oh dear."

"Will somebody please shut that hen up?" whispered Croaky - as loudly as he could. "I can do without the negatives."

"I know what we can do. We 'eggstracted' it before when Verity Vixen tried the same thing," whispered Henrietta, cheekily. "Don't you remember last winter? She executed exactly the same tactics, but we thwarted her. Well - we did lose Dundee the Australian chook along the way, but that was all."

They sat, listened and began to see what she was talking about. They had indeed thwarted that vixen, and she'd never returned. But, you see, Freddie was a determined fox and had been several times, trying to somehow reach them, so far, it had been to no avail. Mind you, eggs had been disappearing, but Farmer Bob seemed not to notice.

Freddie was happy with the way things were going. He heard a few sounds coming from the barn and put that down to hen-snoring and dream reactions. Hens always made noises when roosting, so he wasn't really concerned. Anyway, his hole was starting to take shape.

"Yes, yes," he sang to himself. "Nearly there, a few more digs and I'll be inward bound." The saliva practically swam out of his mouth as he thought about his dinner. He'd be doggy paddling if he wasn't careful.

The Hen Army gathered together all the eggs laid after tea time collection that day inside the barn, and there were plenty. Some small pieces of wood which were lying in a corner, were manoeuvred towards the barn door, and random pieces of rubber broken from a used tractor tyre, were placed underneath each one to form a see-saw. There was also loose dung left behind after sheep-shearing that hadn't been brushed out and gradually hidden behind bales. This was gathered up and rolled into small cannon-type balls. Job done, they settled down around the hole, smiling at each other, waiting in anticipation of Freddie's appearance.

It was 2.00 am. The night was clear and they could hear Olly Owl hooting in the distance. He caught sounds on the wind and flew onto the barn roof to investigate. There he saw Freddie digging for his life in the hard ground under the barn door. He'd no idea if the hens and Croaky knew what was going on, so he flew up to the high window and peered inside. Obviously, they knew: what was he thinking? "Right, this needs the cavalry." He puffed out his feathers and flew off in the direction of the sheep. He landed on the wall near the stables where the lambing shed was built and where, at the back in a small pasture, the grass was luscious, and thirty Herdwicks sheep grazed. Ollie related the situation and, after much consultation and quiet bleating, they began to file through the field one by one, towards the wall surrounding the barn, and quietly waited, watching poor old Freddie digging away under the door, sweat pouring as he sang.

Meanwhile Freddie, totally engaged in his work, found himself tiring. "Yes, yes, look at that hole. Now can I get through it? More importantly, can I get hens out of it?" He gently slid both front legs into the hole and sized himself up. "No, a bit more, that's not quite big enough."

Whilst all this was going on, Shelly the sheepdog shivered, her sleep disturbed. Alongside her lay Mum Lizzie.

Sleepily, Shelley opened her eyes and, gazing into the dimming fire, she nudged her mother. "Wake up mum," she whispered.

"What's the matter, Shelly? Can't you sleep?" She opened one eye and closed it again.

Shelly was having none of that. "Mum, wake up, sniff, listen. Can you feel it?"

"Feel what?" mumbled the old sheep dog. Lizzie sat up, blinked, and sniffed. She sniffed again and listened.

"Yes, I can. Are you thinking the same as me?" She turned to her daughter, moving her mouth, and baring her teeth. "Yes, I bet it's Freddie up to his old tricks again. Come on, let's investigate."

With that, the girls headed towards the back door of the farmhouse. They knew how to lift the latch; it was never locked and there was no-one around for miles. Out they crept, heads down. As they reached the farm gate, some ten yards along the track, Ollie Owl was perched on the wall. They swapped conversations and information, then made their way towards the barn. The barn was to the right of the farmhouse in a separate enclave with the stables next to it. There were also eight goats separated from the twelve-strong piggery, very eager to hear the story. Excitement filled the air, as one by one, all escaped their areas, ready to follow the dogs and Ollie towards the barn. The horses agreed to stay put but, at a signal, would be there if needed. The animals weren't missing this. Life could be dull at times.

By this time, Freddie had created quite a hole and was happy with his hard work over the past hour. He was tired, hungry and thirsty. A trough nearby served his thirst, but he began to feel nervous. He felt his fur stand on end. The moon was shifting, and dark shadows were brooding in this corner of the farmyard.

"Don't be silly," he said to himself, calmly trying to abate his alerted senses. "Everyone is asleep and so is this lot. All I've got to do is get in, grab whatever I can and get out. Then back to my den with dinner." He grinned, nevertheless, he still felt a bit nervous. "Well, there it is. Come on, Fred. You've just got to get in, grab and get out," he reiterated to himself.

Meanwhile, poor unsuspecting Freddie had been so busy concentrating on his project that his senses were letting him down. He had no idea his antics were the focus of attention. He didn't even smell danger - not good.

Freddie was just halfway into the hole where the inside of the barn was in sight. He struggled, trying to get further, wishing he'd made it that little bit bigger, it wasn't easy to move. "Yes," he thought to himself, "just a little bit more work, then home with a Henny Penny."

Just when he was feeling oh-so pleased with himself, the most unimaginable thing happened. He heard the shriek of "Let him have it, girls!"

He looked up, mouth wide open in shock as his face was bombarded with eggs, splattering all over his fur. Freddie's open mouth managed to top the chart with the number of eggs he was forced to catch. He gulped. Obviously, he liked eggs, but four in one go was a bit much. He was choking. The girls were having a breeze. They'd never enjoyed themselves so much since the last time, jumping onto the sea-saws, flicking eggs and dung onto Freddie. After managing to clear the yolks, shells all over, he held his head up again to complain but wasn't quick enough, and nearly choked again on some dung, thinking to himself, "Now that really was a bad egg!"

Croaky was jumping up and down, giving orders and standing at the back as usual, just so he could be seen taking charge of the situation. He liked the thought of being number one.

Now the part of Freddie's body which was on the outside of the barn door suddenly felt extremely painful. Two sheepdogs had ploughed their teeth into his backside and a tumultuous howl came from deep down in Freddie's lungs, spitting out all the gunge he'd been trying not to swallow. The sheep had made a half-moon ring close to where he was straddled, and Ollie was perched ready to fly down and attack Freddie's head when the fox retreated from his bunker.

Freddie's head and fur remained covered in sheep dung and eggs. He was trying his best to retreat, wondering what was making his backside so painful. Shelly and Lizzie were ready. Freddie backed out of the hole into the yard. The fright could be seen in his eyes. He cowered. Laughter echoed all around, such a sight was he, covered in eggshells, yolks, the lot, spitting out dung and wiping his mouth with a paw. He saw the pigs, heard them grunting, heads down, along with the horned goats. The dogs were his worst nightmare. Just a small distance away from his nose, he could see and feel them panting, hot breath rising in the cold night air. For once in his well-heeled life, he felt fear, realising the surrounding sheep were in control. He'd never been so humiliated.

After many threats to his foxy persona, Freddie realised that he'd have to find some other farm to raid, well away from this one and where they didn't know him. The animals glared, moving slightly towards him. His pace quickening, with shoulders and head down, sticky and dripping, he sidled away, heading towards the stream in the valley for a wash, Ollie's ferocious beak still having a go at his head.

Everyone was cheering and thanking each other for their efforts. All the animals did what they could to make sure the hole on the outside was filled in with soil and anything else available. The hens organised by Croaky filled the inside part of the hole with straw and the armaments of war. They all hoped Farmer Bob would take notice of the area when Shelly and Lizzie brought it to his attention the next morning. Everyone went back to their sheds and fields. The dogs crept back into the farmhouse, and all was quiet. Ollie continued on his rounds of hunting and hooting, keeping a grim eye on Freddie's movements for the time being, whilst Croaky, who was very pleased with himself over the outcome, strutted back towards his sleeping quarters.

"Yes," he commented to himself, loudly enough to be heard, "I did a very good job there." He paused to look at the roosting hens out of one eye: they were settling down to snooze, making their little noises. They'd had enough excitement for one night, they were shattered.

"Yes, you see it's all down to strategy. I'm always good at that in such circumstances," Croaky boasted as he hopped onto his bale of straw, positioning himself. He fell asleep in no time with a smile on his face. It wasn't as big as those on the faces of his girls, or the goats, pigs, sheep, sheepdogs, and the still watchful Ollie!!

Suddenly a big kerfuffle came from the top of the haystack. Croaky had fallen off - couldn't quite grip the straw and being so tired, he wasn't positioned properly.

The usual mayhem resumed as hens don't like being disturbed; guttural noises, gentle squawking until Lulu Light Sussex started to squawk more loudly, "Oh, Freddie's not *back* is he?" She fluttered around her hay bale.

"Of course not, you silly gal. Do go back to sleep. You know I'm here to look after you," grumbled a supercilious Croaky.

Lulu smiled at his pompous remark. Crooning sublimely, they all settled down. Then Lucy Hamburg piped up; "Hey girls, "What's the similarity between a cracked bell and a cow pat? Oh, come on this is right up your barn side!" Murmurings, snoring, gentle crooning.

"Oh, for heaven's sake Lucy, aren't you the least bit tired?" shrieked Susie Sussex.

"Oh well, go on then gal, be quick, what's the answer, eh?" Croaky spluttered trying to scramble back to his perching spot.

"Well, you've all dealt with it today," cried an excited Lucy. She waited, then couldn't hold out any longer. "***Dung!***"

She waited for the response; silence reigned. Some chortled, others sighed with an 'oh not again!' 'Go back to sleep' was one of the more polite answers: they'd had enough for one day.

"Huh, that went down like a cracked bell. My best joke too. Such a boring lot." Mumbled a deflated Lucy.

As for Freddie, he was still trying to wash off his fur, the sticky, slimy white of the eggs and the deep yellow of the yolks. Was he in a mess? Oh yes!!

His bum hurt too when he sat down. This was going to take all night. He wasn't at all happy with this outcome and he was even more hungry! Eventually, when he could move without sticking to the ground, he lay down by the stream wondering where he'd gone wrong!

Two Weeks Off

P Wright

Two weeks off work? I was dreading it. I should have been looking forward to a bit of R&R. I used to love holidays, but that was four years ago. Now I am divorced and moved back in with mother. Don't get me wrong. I love her and she has been so kind to me these past four years. But the thought of going to garden centres, bingo, shopping centres and visits to Mom's sister, Vera, felt very daunting.

Daisy, a pretty girl on my team at work, asked where I was going for my holiday. In the past I'd told her I was saving up for a deposit for a flat and that was true. But this year I just couldn't face two weeks at home.

On Fridays after work, I took myself off to the shopping centre, then to Luigi's Italian restaurant. I felt bad at first, telling mother I would be going out for a meal on Fridays with the girls from work. I would ask Daisy if she fancied it, but she was like everyone else who all wanted to get home to husbands, kids or boyfriends. Who could blame them? After feeling embarrassed eating on my own for the first few times, Carlos, the waiter, would greet me and make a fuss. "I have saved you a table by the window," he would always say. Tonight, before going into the restaurant, I paused at the travel agent's window, next door to Luigi's. I made a decision to go inside and browse exotic places and collect a few brochures.

Carlos greeted me and escorted me to my usual table. I placed the brochures down. "Ah, deciding on a holiday. You should visit my beautiful Italy. It is fantastico! I wish I could show you all the beautiful places."

Secretly I thought, 'Yes, I wish you could too!'

Arriving home, I put the brochures on the coffee table. Mom immediately picked them up. "Oh Marie, how fabulous, we're going abroad. I must check my passport. What a lovely surprise. I'll see if our Vera wants to come as well!" she said excitedly, smiling from ear to ear.

How can I tell her I want to go alone? Of course, Aunt Vera will come, if she thinks it's free. There goes a big chunk out of my savings. I thought. Feeling depressed, I put on my headphones, connected them to my laptop and brought up pictures of Italy, deciding this was the place I wanted to go.

Mother had other ideas. "Spain, I think. Look at this hotel, Marie, in Benalmadena. It's got a spa and everything. Nice and flat as well for our Vera. She's not walking so well now since she's had her hip done."

"Mom, I was thinking I would like to go to Italy."

Mom didn't let me finish. "Oh no, too hilly for our Vera. I think it should be this one. You book it and I'll ring our Vera." There was no discussion or compromise with Mom.

That was it, no more conversation. Mom went into the kitchen to ring Aunt Vera. I was still looking at pictures of Rome. Of course, they wouldn't like walking around all the places I wanted to see - poor Aunt Vera's legs. I said goodnight and went to my room, leaving Mom enthusing about the holiday to her sister.

After a week of listening to Mom and Aunt Vera, I really had had enough. I was paying and I had no say in anything. I shouldn't have mentioned it to Mom, then on the other hand, I would have felt guilty.

The following Friday as usual at Luigi's, Carlos asked if I had booked a holiday. "Bit of a problem. Mom and her sister want to come with me. They want to go to Spain and I want to go to Italy."

Carlos sat across the table from me. He put his hand over mine. "This is your time, Marie. Go to Italy, see Rome, Sorrento, and all my country has to offer you. You never know - you might even meet the man of your dreams," he said, smiling as he stood up. "I'll fetch your usual wine. Think about what I've said."

That night, I couldn't sleep and when I did, it was dreaming about the Colosseum, the Trevi Fountain, the Forum, the Palatine Museum, the wonderful statues and buildings, imagining myself in a piazza sipping coffee with a handsome man.

The next morning, Saturday, Mom asked where I was off to. "Just going to book the holiday," I told her.

"Don't forget to get all the seats together," she shouted after me.

Walking to the travel agents a thought entered my head. Three of us sharing a room, me on the sofa bed, Mom and Aunt Vera snoring in unison, bingo in the afternoons, complaining about the heat and sunbeds.

My head screamed! No! I couldn't do it! As I entered the travel agents I asked, "What do you have for Italy? For one."

Lost and Found

Jean Atherton

Fran angrily flicked her mucky duster in the air. She was happy as a cleaner and described herself as a good worker. If truth be known, she was continually late, and her employer had lost count of the number of complaints about her work. Her manager had called her into the office. Fran could tell by the look on Helen's face that this was going to be a happy meeting.

Helen relayed her boss's instructions to Fran. They no longer required her services.

Fran was shocked. She wasn't expecting that. Her temper nearing boiling point, she stood in front of Helen with the bit between her teeth,

"You lot, you make me sick. You stand there all hoity-toity, and you're nowt but a stuck-up bitch, a bitch that's risen from the depths of the slums. Your fancy clothes don't cover up the real you. Think I don't know about you and old stinky Stanley? Working late my foot! You've crossed a wrong 'un when you crossed me!"

After this last remark Helen started to panic, "I don't know what you think you know, Fran, but you can't go around making false accusations."

"False indeed! False, are they? Well you've nowt to worry about then. Gimme me wages so I can get out of this sh....ole,"

"No need for that language Fran. Listen, this is not my decision. We've always got on. There's no need for us to argue. I have to do what the owners say, that's my job. Just give me time and I will find you another position, I promise."

Fran stood there, arm extended, fingers motioning for her manager to place the wage packet into the palm of her hand.

"Okay Helen, I know it's not your fault, I did go on a bit and I'm sorry. It's just that I need the money, I'm struggling as it is. Our Alfie is only on minimum wage. I admit I should have been a better timekeeper, but I had to give the young uns their tea before I ran to catch the bus."

"I am truly sorry, Fran. I know how you've had it hard since Ben left you. If there's anything I can do to help you, please come to me. I meant what I said, "I will look for a job for you."

Fran moved forward and put her arms around Helen. "Thanks love. I appreciate it."

They parted on good terms, but that didn't help Fran. She now had to tell the children that they would all have to pull their belts in.

The next morning, she went to the benefit office and filled in form after form after form. They did hand over a small amount of money, telling her that it was a loan, and she would have to pay it back once her benefit had been sorted.

This was a blow to Fran. She had never felt so low. She found the need to ask for benefits shameful.

Fran was a very resourceful woman, and she did manage, even though it was a struggle. She made meals that were filling rather than healthy. It was a case of bread with this and bread with that, but they managed. She applied for numerous jobs but was always pipped at the post by a younger person.

Then, out of the blue, Helen rang her. "Fran, I think I've found a job for you. Meet me at the railway station at 2 o'clock this afternoon."

Suddenly Fran was full of life, excited even. The thought of earning some money filled her full of hope for the future.

The station was only a five-minute walk away, so she didn't need money for the bus fare. As she approached the automatic doors, she could see Helen sitting in the cafe just inside the entrance.

Helen jumped up to greet her. "Sit down Fran. I'll get you a coffee." She placed the mug of coffee in front of Fran.

"How are you, Helen?"

"I'm fine but how have you been Fran?"

"Oh, you know. I've just got back from a holiday in Portugal, two weeks in the sun. I've booked another in Spain for next month."

They both burst out laughing, "Always the joker, Fran. I've missed you. So have the other women. I had a word with the boss to try and get you your job back, but he was having none of it."

"Thanks for trying, Helen. I have been applying for any number of jobs, but so far, no success. My sister says if a job comes up with hours that don't fit in with the kids, she will sit with them until I get home. That will give me a better chance of getting a job, hopefully."

"That's good to hear, Fran, because I think I have a job for you. That's if you want it. As you know, my Freddie works for the railway, and he told me that this station is looking for a woman to work in the lost and found office. What do you think? Would you like to go and speak to the Manager about it?"

"Would I? It sounds perfect, and on the doorstep."

"Freddie thought you would, so he took it upon himself to speak to the manager about you. He has agreed to see you today. He said anytime would be okay. You just need to knock on the office door on arrival."

Fran jumped up, "What are we waiting for then, show me the way, Helen."

Helen was so pleased to see the old Fran back, "They need to fill the position quickly, no qualifications needed, just a friendly disposition, trustworthy, able to deal with the public." Helen could see that Fran was excited. "Sounds as though this is perfect for you, Fran. You're good with people. I'll take you to the office when you've finished your coffee. They haven't advertised it yet, so you should be in with a good chance."

Fran was too excited even to finish her coffee. Helen walked with her to the office.

"I'll wait for you on that bench over there. Good luck, Fran. Knock 'em dead, gal."

Forty minutes later, Fran was walking towards Helen with the biggest smile across her face.

"Yes. I've got the job. Start tomorrow morning. He even told me they will work around the kids' school hours so I can come in at 9.15 tomorrow instead of 9.00. I'm going to get my uniform tomorrow."

She thanked Helen once again and told her she will not let her and Eddie down. They said their goodbyes and promised to keep in touch.

That night, Fran prepared for the next morning. She set the alarm for 7.00 am which would give her time to do what was needed to get the children to school. The next morning, Fran was up and ready, even before the alarm went off. With the children on their way to school, she made her way to the railway station to start her first shift.

A rather red-faced, portly woman was waiting for her outside the lost property office. "Hiya luv," she greeted, "I'm Nel. Come to show you the works."

She opened the door to display rows of shelving packed with lots of different items. "Good lord!" Fran said, "You wouldn't think people were so lackadaisical. I'd know straight away if I'd lost anything."

"So would I. Some folks have too much money. You'd be surprised at what people leave behind. Anyway, come in, I'll show you what's what." By lunchtime Fran had the job under her belt.

As the weeks passed, she had become very efficient at running the lost property office and she loved it. "It's like being me own boss," she told her sister. Her hours were 9.00 am to 5.00 pm, and her sister sat with the children until she arrived home from work. Fran gave her some money at the end of the week. The arrangement suited everyone.

One day she was sorting out some new items and her back was to the window, "Hello there," a man's voice said.

"Just a moment, sir," she said. "Lost and found Frannie will be with you in a moment."

All of a sudden, he filled the office with laughter. "What a very apt name," he said.

She turned around to be met with the bluest eyes she had ever seen on a man. "Hello sir, how can I help?" She was stuttering and stammering, slightly embarrassed. She was wondering why she was acting like a silly schoolgirl, and mentally told herself to 'Get a grip'.

He told her he had left his laptop on the train, and gave her the time and departure station. She very quickly located his laptop and handed it over to him, obviously after he had signed the Returned slip.

"It's a good job some folks are honest," she commented.

"It certainly is, and thank you so much. Oh, by the way, are you free one evening? After you finish work, of course?"

It didn't take Fran too long to reply as she liked the look of him.

They agreed to meet the following Friday. Coffee in the cafe, a bun and a chat. Fran had never been so happy. It had been a while since she had been in the company of a possible suitor. She felt like a teenager again.

◇

Now one would be forgiven to think this story ended with Fran settling down with Mr. Laptop, NOT SO!!! Turns out he was married with three children, so he received his marching orders from Fran.

Poor Fran, she thought she had found a man friend, but she had lost him just as quickly.

She picked herself up and threw her energy into running a very efficient lost and found office, she loved it.

Herod was Completely Misunderstood

Annette Phillips

Everyone was restless in the field and there was a feeling of excitement mixed with anxiety in the autumnal air. They were leading up to a big day, but what exactly, no one knew. Betty saw there was rather a crowd over by the large oak tree, pecking and scratching amongst the fallen leaves, it was a place good for insects and worms. She could see someone, maybe a passing visitor, had scattered seeds as well.

The farmer, Matt, was very careful now about allowing anyone close to them and there were various slabs of disinfected sponges on access lanes around the farm. Their leader had told them it was to try and ensure none of them got sick. He said it would be catastrophic for them and for the farmer. It was called avian flu and 47 million birds had died from it around the world this year. She could see him now, down near their coop, trying to keep order and herding some of the jennies inside as rain was threatening.

He was a fine, resplendent fellow with his bronze plumage, and quite statuesque. The farmer called him Herod. Herod himself said it meant 'hero'. The farmer and his attendants had given them all names. Although he was a Devon bronze and the biggest, he often had to square up to Chuck, a Wirral black who liked to schmooze up to the females.

Betty kept out of the way or both of them. She and her friend Gabby would often eat away from the others or nestle in the grass and look longingly through the fence netting to the trees and wood up on the hill which bordered onto the open countryside. Gabby had raised a couple of poults, but Betty thought she must have a problem with her laying mechanism as she hadn't had an egg fertilised or seen it grow, a disappointment.

The skies were growing darker, and the visitors were scuttling back to their cars as large drops of rain fell quickly. All the birds were looking around nervously. Herod started making low pitched sounds, his throat and beard rattling, and flapping his bronze wings. It was time for them to hot-foot it back to the large warm coop. Matt appeared squelching around in his wellies and overalls.

"Come on, me beauties, in you go now. Got to keep you warm and dry for the big day."

There he goes again Betty thought, the big day. If Herod knew what it was, having been around the longest, he wasn't letting on.

It seemed to rain nonstop for days, seemed like weeks although it was difficult to tell in turkey-time. Betty looked forlornly out through the wire netting windows. The field was flooded, she could see large sections under water, like a lake. 'Pestilence and flood,' she thought, 'what's going to happen next?'

Something did happen which was a bit of a surprise to Betty, while hunkering down in the nest box filled with warm straw, she had a strong urge to push really hard. She felt something big and firm release. She stretched her legs and looked down in the hay and there it was - a smooth, mottled brown egg. She sat down again quickly.

She had steered well clear of Chuck and Herod …. so, how had this come about? It wasn't until a couple of days later that she told Gabby who was much more experienced in these matters.

"How did it happen, Gabby?"

"I've heard of it before," she replied. "It only happens rarely. An egg of a female turkey will spontaneously develop into an embryo, and then into a baby turkey, which is always male. It's called parthenogenesis." She seemed proud of her knowledge, "I'd keep it quiet if I were you, don't think that Herod would be all that pleased!"

So, she did, she went about her business, sat on the egg until it hatched and her little one emerged looking a bit gummy and bedraggled. He was a bit bemused with the outside world but soon got the hang of things and when the water in the field subsided was soon playing with all the other poults.

The biggest surprise was Herod - he didn't seem to mind. He had always shown Betty respect, he even moved other turkeys and jennies out the way so she could get to the farmers freshly scattered seeds with her poult.

The rumours increased that the big day was nearly upon them. The farmer was often around the field now looking at them all, pointing, giving instructions to the attendants, making notes in books, often sitting them on machines. Betty was snatched at one point away from her poult and put on it and figures were shouted.

A cold crisp winter morning dawned, the smell of snow in the air. Herod was parading around the field telling them that, as a treat, they were going to spend the day inside the relaxing dark where they could be calm and have a bit of a rest before the big day. Gabby heard the farmer Matt say to Herod, "Well done," when the deed was accomplished, and they were all inside.

"Thank you old fella, another successful year, think we'll spare you the chop."

The big day came, they were all a bit dopey and disorientated, suddenly exposed to the light again.

The attendants started herding them down a tunnel covered in straw to a large shed.

"Don't worry about the poults. We will pick them up later," one attendant said to the other. What happened next was a blur. Everything was fast and haphazard like a dream.

All Betty remembered was Gabby saying to her, "Run for it, run for it," as they careered up the field with Betty's little poult between them, then through the netting where miraculously, a hole had appeared onto the brow of the hill and into the undergrowth of the wood where the three of them now lay crouched, hidden.

"He asked me to save you and the little one, did that Herod. He told me what the farmer intended, that we were all to be Christmas dinner. Our necks wrung in that big shed and chopped, when we came from the dark room. He told me of the gap in the tunnel and hole in the field perimeter fence. In fact, he might have sacrificed himself as the farmer has to make up the weight of us two for the orders."

It was hard for Betty to take it all in, but after a while she said, "He lived up to his name - Herod, meaning hero."

◊

Jenny Jones was flustered. The kitchen was hot, and she always felt everything needed seeing to all at once. The pots were steaming, and she had just taken the turkey out of the oven to baste it.

"How long is your mother staying, Jen?" said John, a pint of something clutched in his hand. "Hope it's no longer than a couple of days. I would cheerfully wring …."

"Don't start! Can you give me a hand instead of anaesthetising yourself with alcohol? What's Amy going to eat? She said she couldn't eat something which had a name."

"Yes. He said that one," nodding towards her pan, as she held the basting spoon poised over the turkey, "was called Herod, can you believe? Unless I completely misunderstood."

"Herod is a great name." Alfie appeared at his father's elbow. "I looked it up and it means hero. Can I have Amy's share of turkey, Mum? He must have been big. There's a lot of him

Fly-by-Night Email

Bob Mynors

With huge, grovelling apologies to W H Auden

Fly-by-night email, trashing all borders,
Bombarding mail-order moguls with orders.
Cheap frocks and coats, handbags and hats,
Trinkets and trainers and other such tat.
Exploiting workers in countries afar:
Destined for landfill, it's all so bizarre:
Once what you spent was a mark of your taste:
All you need now is get noticed in haste.
Look in your spam. What do you find?
Emails that never engage with your mind.
'Hey Jack. Do you think you'll please all the Jills?
'You will if you buy our new untested pills.'
'Fortunes await if you'll just send your details.'
'Buy all this stuff for much less than it retails.'
All this takes place like we're still not awake.
Energy drink bubbles: society shakes.

Stay hopeful. Not all is doom.
These screens can lift up the downcast
Towards family, learning, new aspirations,

240

Towards a wealth of information, wealth of
    earnings.
Hanging bright in the sky like gigantic magnets.
A whole world awaits them.
In shanties, favelas, townships,
Souls ache for data.

SMS thanks, info from banks,
Txts of joy from girl and boy.
Photographed meals, or invocations
To slag a celeb without provocation.
And pictures of lovers in moments of passion.
And life-long reminders of ill-chosen fashion.
And gossip, gossip from all the nations.
Bad news financial, fake news insubstantial.
Photos of kids that will soon make them cringe.
Mad drunken faces out on a binge.
Updates from friends with whom you never sat.
Complaints from some scumbag who calls you a
    twat
When a picture you post makes his girlfriend look
    fat.
Slapped down in boxes intended to dazzle,
In pink, white, blue, violet shades of vajazzle.
Intensive, extensive, expensive, offensive,
There just to make others feel apprehensive.

Agents provocateurs, plain liars and trolls,
They spit out their venom and wrong-spell it all.

Millions follow like sheep,
Bleating, like terrified babies,
Of not getting coffee in Costa or Starbucks.

Like sheep on zero-hours contracts, like sheep with
    student loan baggage,
Like sheep in fields not their own,
They cling to their dreams,
But shall wake soon and hope for data,
Though none will relish the friend-counter's
    downward click
Without a saddening of the heart,
    For who can bear to feel themselves deleted?

Warehouse

Graham Bloodworth

The journey had been a short one. All I could hear was the soft tick-tick of the cooling engine.

"Right Sofie, you stay in the van while we sort out some business."

I trusted my older brother and his mate, well sort of. Jason was a chancer; a natural survivor. He took risks that earned enough to put food on the table. As the lads got out of the white flatbed van, just before the doors closed, I called out, "Be quick. Dad will be furious if we're late."

"Quick in-and-out, just looking the place over." He grinned at me, so I stuck my tongue out.

My brother let down the tailgate and collected a canvas bag containing the tools of his trade. The sort of tools that would get both charged with 'going equipped' if caught.

I sighed, watching as they made their way over the broken bricks and other rubbish scattered across the yard, and they were soon out of my sight.

This job had come about, like most, through a chance conversation over a pint. Kevin, the old git who sat in the corner nursing a pint that could be made to last all afternoon, had a story. The cost of this bit of a golden opportunity was three pints and a whisky chaser if it paid off.

"You see lads, back in the day I worked in recreation."

Jason smiled. "You were a bloody parky, you silly sod."

"I know where they put them." He paused long enough to take a sip of his benefactor's pint.

The old council warehouse had seen better days, its windows boarded up, doors barricaded. Walls a riot of multi-coloured art - generally down at heel. It took skill to climb up to the first floor and onto a flat roof. The door to the roof, although closed and with an ancient lock fitted to decaying wood, stood no chance against the wrecking bar's strengthened bite of case-hardened steel.

"Bloody hell mate, it stinks." Jason's nose wrinkled.

Both lads made their way down a corridor, one of many openings that led to offices that now only the ghosts of employees past haunted, stripped of any useful content.

"Nothing up here. I bet that old bugger lied to us."

"Be fair. They would not be up here - far too heavy." Jason started down the corridor, through the remains of a door frame, down the stone steps to the warehouse proper.

The door at the bottom held up against the assault of the bar, yet the last of the nails pulled out of boards like rotten teeth. Jason kicked the remains inward with his boot, and the bang echoed across the dark empty space. He placed the bag on the floor next to the door frame, opened it, placed the bar back in and pulled out a torch.

"Smells even worse down here. How can you stand it?"

Sophie's brother laughed. "Breathe through your mouth."

Puddles splashed against boots; darkness mocked them as the fading light of evening fought against moss-stained, neglected glass in the roof.

From Jason's hand a beam of light danced, Jedi-Knight-style, ready to fight the Evil Empire of a government that did not care.

"Come on. What's that pile over in the far corner?"

As they both approached the ancient tarpaulin covering, Jason knelt to grab a rope handle.

"Come on. Give us a hand. It's bloody heavy."

The tarp gave up the struggle, tearing as if caught on a heavy object. Jason fell on his arse, cursing as the dropped torch rolled away.

"Effin 'ell!"

It rolled back, completing its circle, the beam reflecting faded colours. Something moved. Both lads screamed as the object fell over with a bang. Bits of metal flew across the floor.

"Bastard! Tell me you saw it move." Sophie's brother gave a look of disdain.

"Jumpy sod, aren't you? They're made of cast iron."

He walked over to retrieve a lump of metal, part of a mouth with flat teeth once painted white, red tongue lolling over them. Jason retrieved the torch.

"There must be at least fifty here. Wonder why nobody's nicked them before this."

"Come on. Sofie will be panicking. If she phones my dad, we're stuffed."

As they made their way back, a sound echoed behind them. Jason paused, the hairs on the back of his neck rising, an ancient throwback as old as our species. The subconscious warned all was not well, and he made the mistake of turning around. Within the large lump of darkness in the corner, movement in the edge of the beam of the torch - what looked like a leg. Frozen to the spot, he was aware of more appearing as the tarp rippled and slid back, dark silhouettes spreading out.

Still sitting in the van, I was fed up. Opening the door, and climbing down; I felt the cool evening air chill my arms. *My little Unicorn* tee-shirt had been fine while the sun had been up. The scream startled me, inhuman like some animal caught in a trap. Minutes passed, then a shape scrambled over the edge of bricks half falling to the ground, my brother.

"Where's Jason?"

"Shit, he's got the van keys. Don't ask Sofie. Just run."

I kept up with my brother's half-limp half-jog. He sobbed, eyes wet, not my brother - the one not scared of anything. Once on the road with cars passing us, did he slow down? Once home, he went straight to bed, n ot a word about Jason. I tried the light switch. Nothing. We must have used all the emergency credit on the pre-payment meter. Our parents must have gone to the pub. No matter. The fridge offered up some slices of leftover pizza that did not smell off, and washed down with council pop, free from the tap. No point in me sitting in the dark, so I made my way up to bed.

A noise woke me, something tapping at the front door. Good - mum and dad were back, yet no sounds of a night out. No arguments, no singing. Odd. Maybe dad could not find his keys? I got out of bed, the floorboards cold underfoot. Once in my fluffy unicorn slippers, I opened my bedroom door, hand automatically reaching for the landing light switch. Only then I remembered we were out of credit, bum. The tapping sound had stopped, as if awaiting some response. Halfway down the stairs, when my brother's door opened, revealing a shadowy figure of him in his underpants. Cheers for that. Not something a young teen wants to see. Why was he shaking?

"Sofie, don't open it!"

"Does this have something to do with why Jason was not with you?" I whispered back.

"Shit!" We both jumped as a louder bang knocked on the door.

"Don't open it."

"You don't say." I scooted back up the stairs. "I'm going to phone dad."

"Sophie, please don't."

I had never seen anyone in such an extreme panic as my brother at that point.

"What is it? Who's after you? Tell me. Is it drugs?"

Another bang. The whole door frame rattled.

"You don't understand," he whispered, ending with a half sob.

"Right. I've had enough." I marched back to my room and straight to the window, one which overlooked the front door. Reaching up, I unlatched it and slowly opened it to peek out. A malevolent mist swirled by the door. Something looked up. The nearby streetlamp exploded, making me jump, plunging the street and the door into darkness. I closed the window quick handle, locking it closed.

"What did I see? Is it still out there?"

The assault on the door renewed, and we both looked at each other. I grabbed my mobile, pressed the power button. The screen lit up. Yet as I unlocked it and pressed the icon to bring the phone contacts up, the screen flickered and died.

"No."

"Sophie, hide. I'm sorry, I stuffed up. I love you."

With that, he ran back to his own bedroom, and I heard the sound of the bolt on his door being closed. I rushed across to close my door. I dived into bed, under the cover of my unicorn duvet. A wrenching sounded as the door finally gave way, then silence.

Only the sound of my heart, as loud as any drum, steps on the stairs. More a dull thud. I shuddered. "Someone just walked over your grave," mum would have said. Under the covers, I slowly slid down the gap between the bed frame and the wall - safety. Moving my head slightly, I could see through the gap under the bed, hear the sound of my door opening. Was this someone coming to collect a debt? I knew about those who could not pay the loan sharks back. Enforcers, making certain everyone was reminded of the consequences of not paying on time. Holding my breath, the thump of my heart, ice cold fear. A dark shadow of a leg, movement as the shape left my room.

The scream that followed shook me to the core. Hands over my ears, block out the pleading of my brother's voice. Tears flooded down my face, another wail of, "No!" Please make it stop. The silent wish ignored, sounds of something being dragged down the stairs. Then silence.

Time passed as I shook with fright, only to be jolted by another scream, then a shout. "Sofie."

"Mum, I'm up here."

The sound of feet on the stairs, I recognised mum's shoes.

"Sofie, where are you? What the hell happened?"

I emerged like a small creature from its burrow, safe in the knowledge no predators were around. Scrabbling free of the duvet, straight into mum's open arms. The smell of gin somehow comforting, grounding me against the nightmare.

"What happened love? You can tell me."

I opened my mouth to answer, yet all that came out was hysterical sobs. I tried again - nothing. It was as if the terror that had taken my brother had also ripped my capacity to speak of what happened, I don't remember fainting. Coming to on the downstairs sofa, wrapped up in my duvet.

Blue lights strobed through the front room window; the ambulance woman was nice. The doctor could not get a word out of me, I understood his questions, but hysteria shook my small frame.

PTSD, whatever that is. If it's a loop of the screams running over and over and pleading, then I guess I have it. Once on the ward, I dressed in my pink unicorn pyjamas. Near panic came as the ward lights were dimmed, until the nurse turned on the overhead light on my bed and pulled the screens round. A doctor appeared, a sharp scratch of a needle and the feeling of falling.

The hospital bed was a warm comfort yet, in dark medicated dreams, I ran. Whatever had taken my brother was always just ahead, I could never catch up.

A specialist had explained to mum that severe mental trauma could do that. They would keep me in for tests and observation.

The sheer novelty of being asked to choose what I wanted to eat from a menu, the little acts of kindness by the nurses. One such was the TV room, watching cartoons and not scorning them as being childish, even laughing at some of them. I must have fallen asleep in the chair, waking up as the local news came on. My scream long and loud caused the nurse on duty to come running into the TV room. I stood there, hand pointing at the screen.

◊

"More on the main stories in our region. Reports have come in about a failed burglary at an ex-council owned warehouse. Police today sealed off the premises as an abandoned van had been found. The mutilated bodies of two males in their late teens were recovered from the site. A spokesman for the council said, "Although the Estates Department sold off this asset many years ago, it appears a large stock of cast iron playground horses were left in storage and forgotten about. These heavy, metal rides were removed for not meeting health and safety guidelines. It appears that the two males had broken in, and one was crushed trying to remove one of them. Several others were found scattered across the warehouse along with the body of the second male."

Postscript:

There is an urban legend that, somewhere in Sheffield, the many metal bodies of equine playground rides hide in the dark, resenting their abandonment, biding their time, waiting.

The Dance Off

Sue Allott

The salsa music was fast and furious. Couples around the floor were giving it their all. This was the final of the Tidbury Village's Annual Ballroom Competition. This was hard core. Cynthia and Keith had practised so hard for this event 365 days of the year. Cynthia was exhausted; her reception teaching career had brought her to the local school and her beloved class of thirty tiny mortals. Loving them as she did, she found they could be quite demanding. Keith, self-employed, found his business creating leather goods very tiring on the eyes, focusing as he did on a day's hard work. Still, their love of dance always brought them through – together they felt unstoppable.

That was until a certain Gemma and Martin came upon the scene! They were newish to Tidbury, having moved to the village five years ago when they joined the Ballroom Group. After two years, they came to the decision that they were good enough to challenge the champions. Shock and horror were the reactions of the other competitors. But the pair did alright. They'd won the cup for the past two years. They weren't particularly liked. 'A bit up themselves' was the comment of Keith. A few of the other dancers were a little more gracious with their remarks, although they all felt the same. Some of the local shopkeepers weren't happy with their attitude either.

"We've just got to win this competition, Keith," announced a feisty Cynthia. She'd not lived in this village all her life to be taken down by some snotty newcomers.

"Quite agree," Keith concurred, "but I think the answer is upping our dance routines and finding some different steps. You know - a bit more pizazz than usual."

"Yeah, you're right. That's it. We've got four months to go and time to practise, even if we do collapse receiving the cup." Cynthia laughed with glee.

So, the practices commenced with even more vigour. Life became very intense and exhausting, but they slept well and focused on their mission.

"Hmmm," whispered Martin to Gemma one evening. "I could swear that couple up the road,

Cynthia and Keith, are up to something. They seem to be very shirty and shifty about talking these days. I tried to engage Cynthia the other day, but she practically ran into the house, saying she had urgent matters to attend to."

"Have you ever thought she simply might not like you?" Gemma said sarcastically, ever the put-down wife.

"Hang on, old girl. That's not very nice," Martin retorted sullenly, staring at her giggling face.

"Well, at least I get a smile from Keith." Gemma enjoyed watching Martin squirm. "Maybe we ought to have a go at spying on them. What do you think?" Gemma grinned. "After all, we've nothing to lose, and we've done it before." She said this without any remorse.

"Oooh, you wonderful woman. That's it, that's the answer. We'll have to be very careful and devise a plan."

"Well, that'll be down to me as usual, I suppose," retorted Gemma, remembering how she had to execute the last plan in their previous town. It had worked well, and they'd won a coveted ballroom dancing cup. "Let's get started." Gemma meant business.

Time was passing. Cynthia and Keith choreographed their routines and practised with vigour and enthusiasm.

"Do you know? I feel good about this. Don't you Keith?" Cynthia looked lovingly at her husband of ten years. They'd danced together since they were eight years old, eventually won lots of cups, danced well enough together to fall in love, go on to marry and further their careers. Everyone in the village loved the couple. No children had been born from the marriage, but it wasn't ruled out. There was still time. I mean, they were both healthy and fit.

The competition was still a way off, but Cynthia and Keith felt happy and confident about their routines, until one evening when, returning from work, Gertie from across the road came running towards them.

"Oh Cynthia, have you got a minute? I really have to talk to you." She was red in the face and looked quite flustered.

"Well, we've just finished work. It's been quite an exhausting day and we have to practise, Gertie."

Gertie was known as the village gossip, so people did try to take what she said with a pinch of salt, until she was proven right.

"That's what I wanted to talk to you about. You see, oh but, can I come inside? Only I don't want to be seen talking on the doorstep, just in case someone sees us." She hesitated, glancing around her.

"If you insist," sighed Cynthia. She knew it was no use putting her off. Keith put the kettle on, and they moved to the sofa.

"Do sit down. Now what *is* the matter, Gertie?"

Gertie leaned towards Cynthia, looked around her, as if she didn't want anyone to see her and came out with, "I saw someone looking through your window the other night and then another person last night. It's been going on for quite a while. Every time I go to close my curtains, someone dressed in black passes by, just about the time you start to practise in the lounge."

She stopped and looked at them both, accepting her cup of tea. She had managed to gain their full attention and was, therefore, in her element.

"Last night, I decided to creep out of my back door and follow this person. The person stopped,

259

hesitated, looked around and crept up to your lounge window. You hadn't fully closed your curtains, so whoever it was, managed a good look at you both." Gertie looked at them triumphantly.

Cynthia and Keith were horrified and not pleased, no indeed, not pleased at all. "Well, well, Gertie we have spies in camp," said Keith in a raised voice.

"Yes indeed, my dear, and I shouldn't wonder if it's someone who wants to win the competition by fair means or foul," Gertie finished off with aplomb.

"Hmm, who desperately wants to win this competition other than us? I mean, it's our passion," he said feeling a tad uncomfortable. He went on, "It's got to be Gemma and Martin. They are the shiftiest pair in this village, and I bet they'd do anything to retain their champion's cup."

"Yes dear, but what are you going to do about it?" asked Gertie, her excitement rising.

"Gertie, you mean 'what are *we* going to do about it?" Keith leaned over to her with a smile. "We three, Gertie."

"Oh, oh, I say." Gertie grinned. "I can feel my Miss Marple hat coming out of the wardrobe. What do you have in mind, Keith?"

"They spy on us, you spy on them, and you use a notebook to write down all the details. I will alert a couple of friends of mine and all will be revealed eventually." Keith had stood up whilst giving this little speech, but then sat down and gave Gertie a hug. He surprised himself as he'd never felt tactile with anyone but his wife before, but this was special.

"Gertie - off you go. Be careful and we'll liaise daily. You have our phone number and there's a key under the mat at the back door, should you wish to let yourself in before or after our practices."

"Oh, thank you my dears. Thank you for believing me, and I shall look forward to helping solve this little mystery." With that, Gertie gingerly departed from the house, looking all around her, watching neighbouring curtains and feeling herself slip fully into the Miss Marple role.

"Well, what do you think of that, Keith?" asked Cynthia with a fierce look on her face.

"I don't. It looks like sabotage to me. Two can play at that game. I feel really fired up about this. I'm very angry about the whole thing." He strode over to Cynthia, grabbed her at the same time. "Don't you worry, my love, we'll get to the bottom of it."

Cynthia was looking at her beloved husband in a new light. She puckered, liking his passion. This was going to be interesting.

The days passed with discussions of the excellent details from Gertie's little black book and their own bits of sleuthing. They knew this neighbourhood like the back of their hands, so it wasn't difficult to know where to go and how to be nosey.

The contestants were allowed a dress rehearsal and practice night, not normally a common arrangement, but this was Tidbury. Therefore, from the Sunday before the following Saturday's competition, four couples only per night were allowed in the hall, supervised by members of the committee. It was a huge commitment on their part, but they were dedicated enough to give up their time and energy.

On the Tuesday night, it was Cynthia and Keith's turn and, lo and behold, it was Gemma and Martin who joined them, along with two other couples. Was this just coincidence or had someone used a wand of influence? Cynthia and Keith decided that their choreography would be the same as they'd danced the year before, as they knew their new routines completely and could perform these on the actual night. This was part of their plan, but they agreed to dance a couple of hip-hops differently in front of Gemma and Martin.

"Your choreography is certainly different this time, you two." Keith smiled, noticing a few of his steps performed by Martin and Gemma. "Yes, indeed, very different. It's a pity we didn't do something different ourselves, Cynthia." Keith smirked at Cynthia and then at Gemma.

Gemma opened her mouth to speak but thought better of it. Martin looked at Keith and replied, "Yes old chap, we thought we'd better smarten ourselves up." He could feel Gemma tightening her grip on his hands and it was hurting. He realised she was telling him to shut up and that they had better go.

Saturday came and the large village hall was full. Tables were placed around the perimeter and dancers were seated in their allocated areas whilst the rest of the public were in others. Gertie was sitting at the front, sideways on, at the nearest table to the dancers' area. She was keeping her eye on the situation, along with Rory, Keith's policeman friend. The band was playing on the stage and the buffet was displayed at the rear of the hall, near to the kitchen.

One by one, couples were eliminated; Cynthia and Keith were left on the dance floor with three other couples. They were all good but there could only be one couple win. The judges were very impressed with the precision and excellence of dancing this year. Gemma and Martin had danced some of their routines, but had rearranged choreography for others. Now came the time for the salsa.

The couples rose from their seats and walked gracefully out onto the dance floor. The gentlemen looked resplendent in their tuxedos and the ladies delightful in beautifully coloured outfits covered in sequins, pearls and diamante beads. The music began and clapping broke out on all sides. The tune was very catchy, and the audience clapped to the rhythm. This Gemma did not like at all. She'd never enjoyed or got used to the interference of audiences, it put her off. Martin, of course, always the one to follow if she faltered, agreed.

"We must complain to the committee after this dance," whispered Gemma, trying to smile at the crowd.

The music stopped and one of the judges tapped a couple on the shoulder, indicating they should return to their seats. Gemma confronted the committee over the audience clapping, then an announcement was made to ask people to refrain from clapping. Groans and boos could be heard.

Next was the foxtrot. This was a favourite of Gemma's and she rose with confidence, taking Martin's hand, pulling him onto the floor. But the clapping started again after about a minute's introduction. Gemma realised that, even after an announcement for the on-lookers not to clap, it was a grinning Gertie who'd started it off again.

Gemma was aghast to see Cynthia and Keith dance a new routine. How? Why? When? What Gemma and Martin didn't know was that the new routines had been practised at Gertie's house, so what they had spied on was Cynthia and Keith performing a short practice of their old routines in their own house. Clever, eh?

Another couple walked back to their seats and then there were two. It was the quickstep, to which

Cynthia and Keith danced their new routine. This was another one that the other couple definitely had not seen. Gemma was furious.

Now was the tiebreak. The Viennese waltz. The judges couldn't decide. The couples had been allowed a break and, as the buffet was ongoing, they had partaken of a little, just to keep them going.

The couples were together at the buffet table and, just as Cynthia turned to Keith, she felt something cold down her back. Immediately she asked Keith to have a look. By this time, Gemma and Martin had headed for the floor.

"Oh no, Cynthia. There appears to be trifle on your back, from your shoulders going all the way down to your waist. How on earth has this happened? It's got to be that cow Gemma who did it," he wailed.

"Never mind wailing, honey." she replied. "Just get the stuff off as best you can with a cloth. We've got to go out there."

This he did and off they went, wet dress and all.

Gemma and Martin were smirking when they reached the dance floor, knowing how she had executed her plan, but she didn't see Gertie heading towards the committee with her little black book.

The music started; the dancing began. Cynthia was furious. Her dress looked awful at the back; heaven knew what the judges would say. Keith started to talk to her. "Come on honeybun, you've got to keep up with me and don't let that cow get the better of you." With shoulders set back, Cynthia danced her heart out with their new routine. They smiled lovingly at each other.

"Even if we don't win because of your dress, it's still marvellous to be with you." Cynthia glowed at her husband; she loved him more than ever right at this moment.

Gemma and Martin were dancing their usual routine and again, Gemma was furious to find Cynthia and Keith had altered theirs. The music seemed endless but then, suddenly, it stopped. One of the judges walked out onto the dance floor. Cynthia was swirled round by Keith to see what was happening.

A great discussion was taking place between Gemma, Martin and a judge. Gemma's face was the colour of beetroot and Martin's seemed contorted in rage. No-one knew what the conversation was about, but then Gertie walked onto the floor at the invitation of the judge – carrying her little black book. Gertie was spitting, talking about sabotage. Gemma was so angry, especially at her plan being exposed. Her pert mouth, covered in her famous bright red lipstick – 'Red Heart' Christian Dior, she told everyone, when in truth, she went to her local haberdashery store and bought all her toiletries in their bargain basement, cheap, cheap! Oh, how she showed herself up, and the policeman friend of Keith's, who'd been assisting Gertie, was also confirming the accusations. Gemma moved towards Gertie and pushed her with both hands; she fell backwards and was ably caught by the quick-thinking Rory.

"What on Earth is going on, Gertie?" Keith asked.

"Well, my dear," she began, catching her breath. "I made it my business to bring the details of their nasty little plans to the attention of the Competition Committee in the way I thought fit and, of course, your policeman friend has been here with me all evening. So now it is up to the Committee as to how they deal with this situation."

By this time, Gemma was throwing a 'victim' tantrum about a vendetta against them because they were the best dancers. Unfortunately for Gemma and Martin, they were near where Gertie had been sitting and a sudden scream rent the air. Much to the surprise of everyone, Gemma was sprawling on the floor along with Martin, she hadn't let go of his hand.

"What went wrong there Gertie?" asked Cynthia.

"Oh, nothing for you to worry about my dear. Unfortunately, it seems someone's spilt some sherry trifle on the floor and, somehow, Gemma's stilettos found it.

Cynthia turned round at the sound of stifled laughter and realised it was Keith who was holding his sides, trying to be dignified by holding a white handkerchief over his mouth. He mumbled to Cynthia, "Silly cow! Serves her right. They're bound to be disqualified now."

The judge moved back to his podium and tapped the microphone.

"Er, excuse me ladies and gentlemen. I would like to announce that the judging panel have made their decision and the deserving winners of this year's Annual Ballroom Dancing Competition are…….” Here he held his breath, silence reigned for a second, then…….

"Cynthia and Keith will you please come forward to receive your cup, and, might I add, this decision is in no way due to any recent event. You were high on our list from the beginning of the evening. You have improved tremendously. Well done!" With that he handed over the cup and shook their hands.

Keith grabbed Cynthia in sheer joy and gave her a 'film star' kiss, sweeping her backwards. Great cheers went round the room, led of course by their best pals, Gertie and Rory.

Gemma was helped to her feet and limped off the floor, assisted by the ever-gullible Martin, as he flung a sticky strawberry from the back of her dress along with some custard, fresh cream and jelly which was now sliding down her cleavage. She slid along, growling at everyone around her like a grizzly bear.

"My, how that dress will stain!" commented Gertie, with a giggle.

"It's not the only one," Cynthia said. "Look at mine."

"Oh, don't worry dear," grinned Gertie, "with your prize money, you'll be able to buy the best replacement ever."

Keith placed an arm around Gertie's shoulders, laughing and saying, "Come on guys, group hug. How on earth do we thank you both for your support, especially you Gertie?"

"We owe you," they both chorused.

They all had a good laugh and headed towards the buffet.

"Now be careful with that sherry trifle," remarked Rory.

"I know what we can do," Cynthia beamed. "We can invite you both for a meal and I will make *my* special trifle for the occasion, I haven't made one lately with all the dancing."

"Great. That'll do nicely." smiled Rory, licking his lips and giving her a 'thumbs up'.

Martin and Gemma, a month later, stuck a "For Sale" sign in their front garden.

"I suppose they'll try moving on to their next predation," giggled Cynthia.

"Yes," grinned Keith. "But I don't think we have anything to worry about. Once the news of this incident gets out in the dance world, wherever they go to live, the news will have already travelled ahead of them, and their reputation will be well and truly shredded."

Father's Day

Annette Phillips

Pondering on the past
In the dappled courtyard
On a silent Buddhist retreat,
It is Father's Day.
We are quietly eating lunches,
Carefully packed.
Our crumbs fall and a robin hops in.
It is a reminder of you,
Heaven sent.

In the guise of a robin
You have made yourself known to me, when needed.
That first day in the garden of our family home.
As I was desperate for distraction,
Digging a bed of clotted earth.

273

You perched beside me on the fork handle,
Your red breast puffed, intent on a worm?
Calming my intense grief at your loss.

You were there again in the Trescoe garden,
My honeymoon trip with at last a good man.
Maybe on your migratory path South that September
    day.
For a full ten minutes you stopped as we sat,
Hopping between protea and stone,
Angling your head and beak,
Granting your approval.

I think of so many missed opportunities
When we could have said sorry,
Me to you, you to me
And healed the hurt.
Hidden from each other we remained,
Separated by generations of family reserve,
Joined in mutual stubbornness,
Bound by unexpressed love.

I asked the robin in that courtyard,
What are you saying to me now....?
'Let go' was the reply.
What if I let go?
A new way of looking,
At our relationship, the past.
With that the robin flew skywards,
    Leaving me considering.

The Election Trap

Bob Mynors

The stage was all set for one of the biggest political upsets on record, or so the pundits across the TV stations and other media were saying. Nothing more could be done now to affect the result though: the polls had closed and the Great British public had spoken. And once the votes had been counted, the nation would find out what it had actually said

This election had been, the same pundits all agreed, the most bitter and most closely fought General Election in living memory. As a result, the outcome was awaited more keenly than at any other recent time. A very high turn-out had been predicted and seemed to have happened, but exit polls varied wildly, both across the country and within localities

This keen anticipation had its roots before polling day, however, on the day when, almost as one, the major national parties all announced a name change part way through the campaign period, the better to reflect their positions in the political spectrum, so they all claimed, and to

275

clarify their tactical stances too. Most people were baffled when, supposedly, organisations whose histories dated back more than fifty years at least, and at the other extreme closer to four hundred, would suddenly adopt new and, as some said, frivolous identities. It was the topic that filled most of the air-time at a time there were no more serious events or developments that warranted coverage

By now, surely everyone in the country who cared knew that the Conservatives had switched to being the CONTROVERATIVES and laid claim to the idea that, sometimes, it was necessary to make people peer over the precipice and so win votes by actually showing people the worst alternatives. Similar statements were made by the Labour Party which had renamed itself the LOW-BAR PARTY, explaining that it would achieve its social-reforming aims gradually and with small steps rather than in a single swoop. The leader of what were now the LITDEMS (LITERAL DEMONCRATS), once the LibDems, got in on the act too announcing, most brazenly, "We know that breaking the stranglehold on power held by the other two main parties is going to be a devil of a job, but we are not the Literal Demoncrats for nothing. We know we're up to the task." The

GROANS, meanwhile, once the Greens, claimed that they knew the country was bored with its 'save the planet' message, yet vowed to carry on with 'business as usual'. For some reason, none of the nationalist or separatist parties felt the need to indulge in similar behaviour

Inevitably, these highly dramatic and totally unexpected changes fired up the headline writers into more than their usual frenzy. '*No Ambition Reds*' cried the Mail. '*Bosses Bamboozle Britain*' the Mirror exclaimed. '*Even Low-Bar Too High for Trots*' screamed the Daily Express. '*Names Drawn from a Hat*' was The Metro's contribution

A few days later than the other four, even Reform UK donned its own new clothes, rebranding itself REMORPH UK. The 'quality' news outlets all had fun with that one. '*Reform commits itself to change,*' wrote the Guardian, '*now, tomorrow and forever, with its new ReMorph tag. Whatever song you want to hear, they will endeavour to sing it for you. Whatever words you want to read, they will try to write them. Whatever policies you want to see, that's what they will commit to.*'

Quickly though the novelty seemed to wear off. The parade of ministers, their shadows, assorted front-bench spokespeople and other presumably carefully briefed figures continued to grace the morning TV sofas and radio car interviews, though the subject matter strayed back to other issues considered more central to the election - the economy, education, crime figures, defence, immigration and the ageing population. Normal service had, it seemed, been resumed

The lull lasted for approximately forty-eight hours and it went, in every sense, before the storm. Hurricane Lex had spent several days devastating parts of Texas, most of Louisiana and some of Mississippi, before turning south into the Caribbean then east across the Atlantic, losing much of its oomph on the way, though still with enough fire in its belly to cause major problems in south eastern Ireland, north western France and, of course, the south west of England

Controversative social media was full of scenes from Louisiana with messages amounting to 'look how bad they had it'. Low-Bar published a priority list of the approach they would adopt if only they were in power, starting with the most drastically affected places, working downwards. The Groans used it as a hook on which to hang even more condemnation of the world's refusal to clean up its act and slash use of fossil fuels. ReMorph seemed initially to agree with everyone, whilst the LitDem approach was simply to point out the flaws in what the other parties were proposing. At this, ReMorph went to great lengths to point out that the LitDems hadn't a single idea of their own whilst continuing their agreement across the board, no matter what contradictions that entailed

So, the campaign period drew to its end in a fashion that was all too familiar. Thom McDonald, also very familiar, was to anchor the BBC's election night coverage for the second time in his career. He had his team around him and was briefed to the hilt. He arrived at the studio at 8.15 pm, studying the latest exit polls, reminding himself of the constituencies where all the key political figures of the day were standing and checking to see if there were any interesting celebrity stories his producers were likely to spring on him

He knew, for example, that with two former prime ministers standing, he would have to make reference to them and know what to say should either of them lose. He knew that Newcastle-upon-Tyne Central, after being first to declare at the last three general elections, was firmly in the sights of

Houghton & Sunderland South which was desperate to steal a march this time round on its near neighbours

As he looked round the studio, he saw where the tea and coffee facilities were placed, and the drinking water and fruit juice. Sandwiches and chocolate and crudités and cakes were in judicious places too

Then the floor manager gave him his cue. After a short musical sting, he looked, seriously and intently at the camera, and began. "Good evening. It is 10.00 pm on Thursday. Polling stations are being closed and locked. Ballot boxes are being taken to counting centres up and down the country. Soon the country will learn the result of this, the strangest of general elections in general election history." Part of him really could not believe he had actually said that last sentence, but he knew it was what people wanted to hear, so he did not let his thoughts dwell on it. He knew he would soon get into his stride as the procession of correspondents and commentators, party officials and anyone slightly famous who could be coaxed in front of a camera would soon take the pressure off him until the real business of the night began. He knew also that he could rely on the floor crew to look after him and not allow the embarrassment of the 1987 Dimbleby Mars Bar incident to be repeated

When the news bulletin ended at 10.15, he knew that there would be about seventy-five minutes or so to fill before that first declaration, and he prepared himself for the pointless speculation that would precede it. It therefore came as a jarring shock when the monitor screen in front of him, showing the time as 10.43, flashed up the message 'Recount declared in Glasgow East. He was just in the process of asking the BBC journalist on site in Glasgow what could have caused this unexpectedly early surprise when a similar flash announced a recount in Nottingham North, and moments later another in Cardiff Central

Cutting short his conversation with the correspondent in Glasgow, he turned to his colleagues in the studio and asked if they could explain this astonishing turn of events. Heads were shaken all round until one, ending a call on his mobile, was able to relate that the exit polls in all those constituencies had been wildly wrong. Whilst they had all predicted turnouts not unlike previous general elections, the numbers of ballots placed in ballot boxes was down by ninety-five per cent or more. Similar results started to come in from all over the country. Political interviewees were at a loss to explain this bizarre phenomenon, except perhaps to blame it on the negative campaign tactics of their rivals. That attendance at polling stations had been in line with expectations whilst numbers of actual votes cast had plummeted was even more perplexing, Victors were being declared nonetheless, though with votes in numbers that would been seen as perilously slim majorities on earlier occasions – some as low as double figures and perilously few making it as high as four figures

By 3.30 am, a slim majority was declared for the Controversatives, though on all sides, it was being asked what possible authority the house could have with so few people having voted for it. And it was left, eventually, for the King to break with centuries of tradition and issue a statement at 10.30 the following morning asking if it had perhaps not been a mistake for the parties to take the nation for fools by acting in the cavalier fashion they had in the election build-up

The Garden Center

P Wright

After a walk with the dog, on the field at the back of the garden centre car park. Well, I say walk, the dog runs about ten miles and we probably walk a quarter of a mile.

We make our way down the car park, through to the garden centre, to the deli, for our usual cappuccinos, although they could pass for anything really, but they are hot and wet, depending on who is serving. Passing sweet-scented flowers with unbelievable price tags, I always stop to admire a pretty flower and look at my husband, Dave, pleadingly. He always says, 'No, forget it. It will only die, because you never water them." Even though I promised I would, I knew he was right.

Since having the dog, we have been trying to get him use to travelling in the car - just a short drive to the garden centre where he can get his exercise, play with his ball and do his ablutions, but to no avail. After seven years, he still does not like travelling in the car. So we're still going to the garden centre every day, well, unless it's a holiday or an appointment somewhere, which gets more frequent as the years pass.

If we walk down into the courtyard towards the deli, there are always some friends or acquaintances, old and new, sitting under the large umbrella, which neither keeps the sun off or the rain out, all in their usual places. We normally find a shady, dry spot for the dog. Alice sits on her own with Toby, her pug, in the corner, waiting for her friend. I always go over to Alice to have a chat, usually complaining about the weather as we Brits do, stroke Toby and give him a treat out of my pocket. 'Oh Toby, how can I resist those large, beautiful eyes?'

Rose and her husband, John, who used to be neighbours of ours many years ago, sat there. Lucy and Tom sat with them, with their dog Poppy. We had only met them a couple of years ago, but something just clicked between us. We often all meet at the garden centre. They only live ten minutes' walk away from us, and we never arrange to meet: it just happens.

John moved the chairs about so we could all sit together. Dave went in the deli for our coffees. Anyone looking around all of the faces must have thought it looked like a pensioners' outing, all of us over seventy years old. The first greeting was, "How is everybody." I should know better than to ask that by now. Everyone spoke at once. Only Rose was quiet and pulled a face. Years ago, the first question would be, 'How is this weather suiting you?' Not any more. I smiled at Rose and asked softly, "How are you today?" She smiled at me and said something I couldn't make out. She has dementia.

John, her husband, replied for her, "She's doing OK." I asked how he was doing. "Still coping," he replied. John has prostate cancer, but he says it is shrinking, and he looks quite fit although we know he isn't.

Then I asked, "How is your shoulder now, Tom?" Tom was in his eighties and looked pretty fit.

Tom smiled, answering, "The physio has sent me exercises for my knee. I asked the doctor's receptionist, "Do you think they'll work for my shoulder?" She apologised and said they're going to send some more for the shoulder. She said the doctor had looked at my records and the last information was for my knee. I told her to look at the dates.

"Oh yes," she says, "it was ten years ago, you haven't been since, so that will be the mix up." We all laughed at this and had anecdotes of our own to tell about mix ups.

Alice walked over, holding on to her stick in one hand and Toby in the other. Overhearing our conversation, she told us about her recent experience in hospital with a collapsed lung. They were preparing her for chemotherapy, and when she asked the nurse why, she was told, 'Because your name's on the white board.'

"If my daughter hadn't been there to tell them it was the wrong person, I might not have any hair by now!"

I turned to Lucy, "Good job one of us is OK." I told her.

"Well, now you mention it, this tiny spot on my nose, the doctor says it's cancerous. I may have to have plastic surgery, but at my age I don't think I'm going to bother. I'm more worried about Tom. He has been told he has cataracts now and may not be able to drive."

We all fell silent for a second and looked at Tom's eyes as if we could see the cataracts in them.

Lucy asked, "Has Dave heard anything from the hospital yet?"

I leaned towards her, whispering. "Do you mean for his eye, his arse or his defibrillator?" Lucy laughed. "Well, he goes for the camera up on Monday," I whispered.

"What about your knee?" she asked me.

"Still waiting," I replied. "Between us, I think we all keep the NHS busy."

The subject changed as Tom, John and Dave chatted over the latest news, putting the world to rights, what they would and wouldn't do. I asked Rose if she wanted a drink of her coffee, but she said no.

I asked Lucy how her granddaughter's twins were doing,

"We're going up this afternoon to give her a hand. One has bronchitis and the other has an ear infection. It's not just us old ones, is it?" Lucy demonstrates, rocking the babies, one in each arm. "Her mother is home tomorrow from a week in Benidorm, 'with the *girls*' (air comas, 'all in their forties').

I looked around at all us oldies sitting discussing illness, pills and treatments. Only a few years ago, before Covid, we would discuss where we would be going on holiday. Now it's trying to remember all the holidays and places we have been. I thought about when I was in my forties then, I remembered Rose who then lived next door to us, tall, slim, blonde, so attractive, very clever, always with a witty quip. But now this frail lady in a wheelchair, her blonde hair now grey and able only to have short conversations. John, her husband, seemed to have shrunk but put on weight around his middle, the same as Dave. Only Tom had remained thin, a bit too thin probably. John was a handsome man when he was younger, and with Rose made what seemed to be the perfect couple. It must be hard and upsetting for him to see her like this, but the love is still there between them, which is lovely.

I then looked at Tom, such a nice man who always has a joke and never moans. He must sometimes have felt outnumbered with his wife and three daughters in the house, but a good match to Lucy, who was small, blonde and still an attractive woman for her age.

I then looked at my Dave. This was not the man I married. That man was tall, fit, with hair. This Dave had rounded shoulders, found walking difficult, even with a walking stick, and was practically bald. It still baffles me why he needs shampoo! Then I think about myself, when I look in the mirror first thing in the morning. I don't like what I see, wrinkles everywhere and no amount of cream will change them. But then I think how lucky we are meeting these lovely people at our age, practically strangers who are now friends, with whom we can discuss everything and anything from personal problems to holidays to the good old days, from what we are having for tea to the latest news, and we all have our personal problems and views on things.

The dogs, Lucy's Poppy and my Fudge, are whining: they want to go. There are no treats left. Well, we've been here for two hours, so it's time to say our goodbyes and "See you all tomorrow!"

The Stone House Remembered

Sue Allott

On Church Street, it stood, so tall and ornate
The hallowed hub of Saturday's gatherings, where
   my story began
The night I enrolled behind the bar to work late -
At first it was daunting, but I realised how life ran
All round these walls from inside and out.
Voices raise, sing and chant by every man
And woman, who passed through those doors.
Loving the atmosphere of magic and
   conversations
Of laughter, the buzz and spillage on floors We
   laughed with the punters, whose couture was
   ruffled
Desperate to finish their night in this House, to
   reach
Over heads, shoulders and arms, all orders
   muffled.
Then the landlord would shout to all and sundry,
"Drink up you lot and get on your ways, no
   staying
In passages for naughty ways. Don't forget its
   Sunday

Tomorrow, nightclub heads will be throbbing and
    swaying."
Closure came with sighs all around and the big
    doors locked
From courtyard to main house. The bouncers sat
    down
Along with us staff and always my turn, "C'mon
    cock
Take orders for yon Greasy Vera's downtown."
Angie and I to Vera's departed with a list and cash
For burgers, eggs, toms, sausage and bacon,
Returning with the above in an assorted
    mishmash.
It quickly went down and all thirsts were slaked as

Well-trod; helping the punters from all corner
    nations
To enjoy their life with wine, spirits and beer.
Was I good at cocktails? I tell you my friends,
My skills were second to none, and many a cheer
Went off at my post, as the shaker I'd send
Swishing up, down and round, sloshing a Sidecar,
Hawaii, or Singapore Sling, oh yes, my dears, life
Was good in those days; we had such fun then
    hurrah
When it ended and the huge bell rang, the air rife

With last orders, sweaty hands and slurred speech.

We played cards. Those who didn't made lots of
chatter.

We never did leave till early morning. There were
always

People spilling out of buildings with still such a
clatter.

Some of us visited Josephine's, for champagne
and fayre,

It flowed from kind punters, the music was loud,

But oh so good, this really is where, we let down
our hair,

Dancing and singing. It was so good to be out
with our crowd.

Then go home safely in time to share

Some sleep before work, hopefully no matchsticks
lancing

Our poor tired eyes, all self-inflicted, dancing.

On the night before Christmas, landlord set out a
plan,

A fancy-dress theme for the Eve and all staff
would dress

Up in style, joining the punters to show where it
began with

That long journey by shepherds and kings, away
from the mess

Herod created. Okay we all said, job done, we'll
do you proud.
Well, there we were dressed up in tinsel, sparkle
and colour;
Me as a fairy, who nearly toppled the tree, but I
was sound
In my ball gown of white, topped with velvet
black, my hair even fuller,
Backcombed to hold my tiara, and wings on my
back, fixed round
My shoulders. Our faces shunkled, under ceiling
lights.
Suddenly, doors opened wide and mayhem
resumed, cheers and great sounds
From the punters that night, at the shock of us
staff
All dressed up to kill, stopped them dead on their
feet at the sights
Before them, a fairy, a snowman and shepherds in
costumes
All went with a swing, as into the courtyard I
swept
Laughing and prancing with wand to the fore, but
feathered wing plumes
Hampered my style, as the cocktails I sent

Over the bar, somewhat skew-whiff; at every turn
    someone yelled out
"Take the bloody things off,
You'll do yourself damage and give us a clout!"
Sighing heavily my attire was removed, and then I
    was free
To parade around
As a wingless fairy.
Peace was restored,
The night swung with spirits of – well,
Hopefully Christmas, moving my cocktails off the
    back shelf,
Set us a task of dispersing the crowds, but our
    training did tell
Of the speed with which we coped with all of the
    tasks.
A surprise I received at the end of the night, with
    full whack.
I was chosen as best dressed bar staff that
    Christmas.
Our Santa Clause landlord, addressed his large
    sack
And brought out my present then everyone
    clapped. But
On Mistlemass Night, my title had changed from
    the Christmas Fairy

To an Angel who'd fallen! Oh, what a come down
but realised,
Back then, with a simple costume I could have
been Mary!!!

Story true as it's written and more!! That was just one part of the total enjoyment of working at the Stone House for three and a half years of my working life at Royal Hallamshire Hospital then going down town, aged 33 (80s) at tea time. It helped me recover from my second slipped disc. I loved every minute with 'Our Alan' who was a fixture during the day, with front tooth missing and Brylcreemed hair, he then graciously handed over to us young'uns early in the evening. It certainly was therapeutic.

The Stone House basically dated back as a building on Church Street from 1795 – White & Sons, Thomas Aldam is over the archway of the door. It passed through various merchant companies selling wines, spirits and beers. Then over the door was added The Stone House and private lodgings. This appeared in 1913 and was a Grade II listed building

Sadly, the colourful and interesting courtyard disappeared in the 1980s. It was an unusual place with a Tudor-like façade of houses and tiny shops which actually sold watches, clocks from Nick de Nitto's, and a lovely dress shop. The rubbish with which it was replaced thankfully eventually closed.

The building now awaits a loving owner to bring it back to life again.

Every Witch Should Have a Black Cat

Jean Atherton

**"Where the hell has this black cat come from?"
Jack shouted upstairs.**

"How would I know?" Sue yelled back at him, "I'm in the bathroom. I haven't been downstairs yet."

She jumped out of the shower. Intending to go for her morning jog. She threw on her jogging bottoms and t-shirt.

"Sue, come into the kitchen and look at the bloody cat. It's made itself right at home sprawled out on my jumper."

Sure enough, the cat was curled up in the corner, on top of one of Jack's jumpers. "You should have put it in the washer, not on the floor. Look at him, he looks so sweet. I wonder what his name is." she said, bending down to stroke the cat's head.

"I have no idea and I don't bloody care. Get the damn thing off my jumper and out of the bloody kitchen. How the hell did he manage to get in the house anyway?" he grumbled.

"He's a grumpy old sod," she said to the cat. In response, the cat stretched and purred as it raised itself up from Jack's jumper and began rubbing its head against her legs. Then it went over to Jack and did the same to him.

"Get out of the way, mongrel," he shouted. "Sue, get this thing out of the house."

He tried to move away from the cat but it continued to follow him.

"Ahh, look at him. He really likes you, Jack. I can't understand why for the life of me. You're such a miserable old sod. Why don't you just stroke him?"

That's exactly what he did, the cat purred loudly as he moved his head to and fro under Jack's hand, Jack was smitten. He turned and said, "We should get a cat bed for Sooty. It can go in the corner. He obviously likes it there."

She couldn't believe what she was hearing. 'Where did he get the name Sooty from?' she thought.

"Okay," Sue replied, "I know what I can do, I'll put an advert in the corner shop and see if anyone claims him. How did you know his name is Sooty?"

"NO!" Jack shouted, "Leave him where he is for now. He couldn't have liked where he came from, or he wouldn't have run away. I'll call for some cat food on my way back from my jog." As he went through the door his parting words were, "It was the cat, He told me his name was Sooty."

That was that. Sue hadn't at this point questioned the sudden change in Jack's attitude. Still, she was happy that Sooty was staying.

Sooty settled in and they were a happy threesome He loved to sit on the sofa beside Jack, purring loudly as Jack stroked his head.

A few weeks later, Sue's friend, Ellie, popped round for a coffee.

"How have you been Sue? Where's Jack? Is he at work?" she asked.

"No, he's just gone to the shops for some bits for the cat."

"What cat?"

"My little Sooty, you'll love him, He's so adorable. Just walked into our kitchen a couple of months ago and he is still with us. It's as if he's been with us forever. He loves being petted, and he loves Jack."

"Blimey, I didn't have Jack down as an animal lover," Ellie said as she came over to get her mug of coffee.

"No, he never was. Can't understand the change in him. He makes me a drink every morning before leaving for work. Since having Sooty, he's a changed man. I'm not complaining, I love it." Sue reached the biscuit tin and placed it on the kitchen table. "Come and sit down, Ellie. Help yourself to the biscuits."

"Have you no idea where the cat came from?" asked Ellie.

"No idea at all. Jack and I have been trying to work out how the cat got into the house. He wasn't there when we went to bed, but the next morning he was sitting there in the kitchen. It's a complete mystery, but we love him now so, until he wants to return to where he came from, he can stay with us."

Ellie then started to tell Sue everything that had happened since their last meeting. Between them they put the world to rights and two hours later, they said their goodbyes. Ellie went off to get her husband's dinner ready.

It was the last week in October, Halloween was just around the corner. They had decided to have a Halloween party and invite most of the neighbours. Invitations were sent out and most of the neighbours accepted.

On Halloween night, Jack was in the kitchen plating up the sandwiches. Sooty jumped up and ran to the cellar door. "Don't go down there Sooty," Sue shouted.

"Too late," Jack said, "he's already down the cellar steps."

Sue stood on the top of the cellar steps, "Sooty, Sooty, come on baby." Sooty ignored her. "I'll have to go down and carry him back up," she said as she switched on the cellar light. "There you are, you little tinker, come on. I hate being down here." She reached out to pick him up, but he ran over to the back of the cellar and jumped up onto a tin box. "Where on Earth has that come from?" She had never seen this box before. "Jack, is this your tin box?" Sue shouted up from the cellar.

"No. I forgot to tell you it was delivered yesterday by a weird looking old woman. She actually said it was a delivery for Susan Ward. I only turned away for a second and when I looked back, she had disappeared. Sorry love, I forgot to tell you."

"Did she leave a key? Get off the box Sooty. Stop scratching the lid." Sooty was trying to lift the lid but it was locked.

"Sooty, move. It's Halloween and our guests will be here any time." Sooty ignored her and kept scratching at a label on the lid.

"Come on love, hurry up," Jack shouted down.

"I can't get Sooty off the lid," she shouted back.

Sooty had scratched some of the label away revealing a bit of shiny metal. "The key! Sooty, you are such a clever cat." Ripping off the label, she retrieved the key. Sooty seemed to settle. It was as if he had guided her to the box and now she was about to open it. He seemed to settle, sitting beside the box watching as Sue turned the key.

She slowly lifted the lid to display a folded piece of black material. Taking it out she shook it; it was a cloak. She let it drop to the floor. Immediately Sooty went straight to it and sat down on it.

"Well, just look at this," Sue said to herself. Also in the box was a large book with a black cover. The cover told her it was a book of spells. She opened the book at random and found what claimed to be a spell to make people happy. "What a load of old codswallop, Sooty."

She turned to look at the cat, His eyes were lit up like bright green electric bulbs.

Suddenly the cellar door slammed. "Hey, what's happening?" she shouted. "Jack, are you there? Let us out." Thirty minutes later, she was still hammering on the cellar door. Panic was starting to set in. "Jack, open the door." She started to scream, then floods of tears ran down her cheeks.

She was hammering loud, but Jack didn't come to let her out. "Let me out, Jack."

Then she turned to the cat and cried, "This is all your fault, Sooty."

Going back to the box, she took out a bag which contained a witch's outfit. Whilst she was waiting for someone to open the cellar door, she decided to try the clothes on. She was quite surprised at how comfortable she felt in them. She picked up a broom which was leaning against the cellar wall. She then took the wand and swishing it to and fro in the air she chanted,

"Hokus Pokus, Jack's in trouble. He'll open the door to hubble and bubble. Hubble bubble toil and trouble" The words had only just left her mouth when Jack shouted down the cellar steps. "Are you okay Sue? I didn't know you were still in the cellar. The wind must have blown the door to. I was outside in the shed looking for my wizard outfit."

"Jack, thank goodness, I was starting to panic. Come down here and look at what's in the box."

He immediately joined her in the cellar, "You look great in that witch's outfit. You only need a few warts on your face."

Sue went back to the box and, underneath the book of spells, was an envelope which contained a letter.

"Read it, Sue." Jack was smiling.

She started to read its contents out loud. Hello love. Hope you like the contents of the box. Enjoy your Halloween party. Lots of love Mom XX'

"Jack, the box was from my mother."

"I know. Didn't I say a strange woman delivered it?

That evening Sue dressed up in witch's clothes and greeted her guests at the door, sitting by her side was her faithful Sooty.

"Every witch should have a cat like you, Sooty," Sue said to her cat. He purred as he wrapped his body around her legs, then slinked off into the kitchen to sleep in his little bed in the corner.

Eventually Jack confessed that the cat was given to Sue, along with the tin box, by her mother who, by the way, was also a witch and owned a black cat just like Sooty.

If Only …

Penny Wragg

"If only I could have been a gardener," he thought. He gave a deep sigh. There was really nothing he liked better than tramping around outside in his wellington boots and old smelly Barbour jacket, breathing in the smell of dew-soaked grass or marvelling at the intricate patterns made by the early morning frost. He loved every season in the garden. There was always something to alert the senses, always beauty to savour.

At this time of year, the purple wisteria took one's breath away. It looked sensational as it trailed across the honey coloured south-facing wall. The borders around the lawn were crammed with alliums, lupins and forget-me-nots, jostling for pride of place. He counted himself very lucky that he had a large garden which he had nurtured over many years.

One of his favourite corners housed the walled herb garden where scents of rosemary, sage and lavender created a heady mix. The lavender always reminded him of his beloved grandmother.

307

During the enforced lockdowns of the pandemic, he had time to appreciate the many shades of green in nature - who knew there could be so many? The multitude of changes throughout the seasons had struck him afresh, even with one plant alone. Take the viburnum for instance with its deep green corrugated leaves. In June it would erupt with tiny white tubular flowers. In the autumn it would surprise again when the flowers gave way to blueberries.

"Dear me!" he chuckled to himself. He was turning into Alan Titchmarsh or Monty Don. "Wouldn't it have been wonderful to be a presenter on *Gardeners' World*?" He could have written one or two books about gardening, or maybe a history of plants. If only he'd had the time.

He was now at a crossroads in his life. Yesterday he had walked along the avenue to the summer house, under the canopy of lime trees. He always found this had a calming influence on him. His thoughts stopped jumping around in his head and settled into a pattern. He noticed that some of the roses were just coming into bloom. Maybe this chapter in his life would be a late blooming? "If only I was younger," he thought, "and fitter!"

Although he wasn't too decrepit for his age, all things considered.

For all his adult life, gardening had been more than a hobby. It had been a passion. He had squeezed it in whenever he could. His job was very demanding. It is always hard work and a huge responsibility when one is part of a family firm. There is the sense of duty, the pressure to keep everything going and to not let the side down. Now both his parents were dead, it was down to him to run the firm. In a way, he had been waiting for this moment his whole life. It's funny how one never expects it to happen and yet one recognises the inevitability of it all. One somehow thinks one's parents will live forever.

He knew that his siblings would work hard to keep business going as usual. However, he was ultimately the one at the helm, taking the reins, steering the course or whichever metaphor is most appropriate. But if only he could escape and kneel down in a damp flowerbed to marvel at the bees and butterflies, of which there were many. In his head he imagined extending his wildflower meadow……….

His reverie was rudely interrupted…….

"Darling, hurry up. Everyone will be waiting."

For a moment he didn't answer. He held his breath.

"Don't be silly, Charles," rasped Camilla, a Rothman's in one hand and a large G&T in the other. "You know you have to go."

Charles turned and smiled apologetically. He held out his hands in a gesture of submission.

He reached for his Coronation robe.

Desert Island Discs

Bob Mynors

The strains of *By a Sleepy Lagoon* fade away and are replaced by the silky tones of Kirsty Young who welcomes us to the latest edition of *Desert Island Discs*

"Today, we break with *Desert Island Discs* tradition and talk to not a famous film star or musician, not a top sports star, not a leading politician, business figure, scientist or broadcaster – not a human being at all, in fact. Today my castaway is a natural phenomenon, one that affects every one of us every day of our lives. Today my castaway is The Weather

"The Weather, tell me how you went about choosing eight discs to take with you to the island."

"Good morning, Kirsty. Thank you for having me. Well – what I've tried to do is choose pieces that sum up the relationships I have with people, and the ones they have with me. I'm there for people, as you say, every day without fail, whether they like it or not – no pun intended. There's nothing I can do about it - nothing anyone can. I'm just there. Even on days when you people never stir from the little boxes you live in and try to shut me out, you still see me through windows, and often hear me as well."

"So, tell us please what your first record is."

"Well, there really is only one place to start from for me – Vivaldi. The Red Priest has proved a great ally over the centuries. His *Four Seasons* has helped many find ways to cope with all that I am required to throw at them. I know many people nowadays see the piece as a bit of a cliché, as a signal for frustration even, thanks to the way it has been abused in telephone call handling systems, but my selection I think shows this music still has great strength and resonance. It's from *Summer*, in the third movement. It's the bit where the rain just keeps on falling, falling down … where the rain just keeps on falling, falling down."

♫

"And your second choice?"

"My second choice is *Summertime* from *Porgy & Bess*. This is a lullaby, of course. A mother sings it to her baby. But it's also a song about loss and longing. And disappointments. The mother is singing to the child about how beautiful and fulfilled its life is going to be, knowing that exactly the opposite will prove to be the case

"People always associate summertime, what they see as the good-weather time, with happiness, fun, fulfilment. But everyone knows how far from the truth that can sometimes be. This song reminds people that, even in the height of summer, even when their best hopes of me have come true, they may be only a step away from melancholy."

♫

"Round about this point, I generally ask my castaways how they will cope with loneliness on the island, being cut off from contact with other people. Would that even be an issue for you?"

"I suppose you could say that loneliness, in so far as it applies to me at all, is my natural state. I have my allotted tasks and I carry them out according to my own rules – by and large. I do interact with the other elemental forces, of course, both the earthbound ones and those that exist beyond the Earth. The Sun and the Moon – they're both good friends of mine really, but they can lead me a merry dance sometimes. But they've got their jobs to do just as I have, so I can't complain. We do have a good laugh about it sometimes."

"So - record number three?"

"Record number three comes from the Tamla-Motown catalogue – *I Wish It Would Rain* by the Temptations. It's another song about loss – lost love this time. The poor chap in the song has been stuck at home ever since his girlfriend walked out on him. His tears keep rolling down his face. Everyone, he thinks, will look down on him and laugh if they see him crying. So he looks through his window and sees the sunshine and blue skies, and he wishes them away. This kind of weather, beautiful as most people would see it, is no use to him. He wishes it would rain so *raindrops will hide my tear drops,* a*nd no one will ever know that I'm crying - crying when I go outside*. Nice metaphor, I suppose, but it's no way to live a life."

♪

"What about your physical needs, The Weather. Will you be able to make use of what you find on the island to be able to survive?"

"I'm luckier than your human castaways because I feed on whatever I find. I've no need to look for anything specific or watch out for things that may harm me. What is there is what will feed me. It may be that this desert island is an idyllic place with a climate to allow me to put my feet up and have a rest – just enjoy the world as it passes by. Alternatively, it may be that I have to whip up the odd typhoon or monsoon, or even create the conditions for another South Sea tsunami. I don't have any choice in these things."

"What about shelter? Will you be able to deal with that? Do you have the kind of skills you will need?"

"Shelter? You mean from the elements? I can't believe you've asked me that, Kirsty. I am the elements. There's nothing I can throw at myself that I won't know how to deal with."

"You're right, of course. I'm sorry. I really should have thought of that. So tell us about the fourth record you've chosen."

"I think everyone probably needs cheering up a little now after the last couple of choices. But I bet most will be surprised when I say I'm going to use winter weather to do that. Again people automatically associate winter with cold, dark, dreary, depressing weather. But in *Winter Wonderland*, my next choice, even though it's cold, even though it's snowy, everyone is happy. They're so happy they talk about building a snowman and asking him to marry them. Which sounds like a great idea to me. If I had a corporeal existence, I would open up a *Parson Brown's Winter Wonderland Wedding Chapel and Indoor Sleigh Ride* venue in Las Vegas. I'd clean up."

♫

"So, The Weather, we're halfway through. What do you have lined up to take us into the second half?"

"My next choice, Kirsty, is a piece that I don't think many of your listeners will be familiar with. It's called *Volcano for Hire*."

"Volcano? I wouldn't have thought volcanoes count as weather. They're not – atmospheric enough."

"Oh, you are right, Kirsty. Absolutely. I get involved on the fringes of volcanic activity sometimes, when all the fumes and dust particles get thrown up into the atmosphere: I do have to take responsibility for that. But no, in any sensible reading of the situation, volcanoes are nothing to do with me. I leave them to my colleague Mother Earth: they're her problem. But I'm including this track for two reasons - first because I like it, but mainly because it is by a band called Weather Report. Is that OK, Kirsty?"

"I suppose so, The Weather."

"Thank you."

♫

"So where to next? What's your sixth choice?"

"*Volcano for Hire* obviously took us up into the mountains and we're staying there for my next choice, though with a much happier weather outcome, I hope. The song is called *Mountain Greenery*, and before you ask, I'll tell you that I am all over the lyrics. It begins *In a mountain greenery where God paints the scenery, just two crazy people together.* But it goes on, *While you love your lover, let blue skies be your coverlet. When it rains, we'll laugh at the weather.* And if there's not enough weather for you in the song itself, I shall just remind you that my chosen version is by an American jazz singer called Mel Tormé. Mel had such a great nickname. Like Springsteen is *The Boss,* Elvis *The King,* Sinatra *The Governor* – Mel Tormé was *The Velvet Fog. The Velvet Fog.* That makes him definitely one of mine."

♫

"Very clever. The next thing I want to ask you about is escape. Will The Weather try to escape from the island, or will you just accept your lot and stay put?"

"Well again, it's just not an issue for me like it would be for your human castaways. There's the old Butterfly Effect on my side, for example. I don't know who thought that name up, but it's a bit harsh – blaming poor little butterflies for all the work I do. But one way or another, butterflies or no, I shall still have my global reach no matter that

I may be stuck on an island somewhere. Why would I worry?"

"So – choice number seven?"

"We're back to another broken-hearted young man with this one. The song is *The Rhythm of the Rain* by The Cascades. I do have to wonder sometimes about young people's attitudes to me – especially young men. I see them walking out in the coldest conditions I can conjure up wearing just t-shirts and jeans, being all tough and macho. Then, at the slightest hint of a romantic setback, they churn out songs like this one. It goes, *Listen to the rhythm of the falling rain telling me just what a fool I've been. I wish that it would go and let me cry in vain and let me be alone again*

"I mean, come on. Do I look like the kind of force of nature that has time or inclination to taunt every silly young man who's been too inattentive or unimaginative to hang on to his girlfriend? They should just get over it. But it's still a pretty little song, so I thought I'd put it in."

♫

"We've reached choice number eight, your final choice. What delight have you saved up for us?"

"Something strong, I thought, something quite strident to end with, that speaks of the weather people don't like, weather they don't look forward to. But whether they can take action against if they choose which I think makes it hopeful. The kind of weather that, with hat pulled down and collar turned up, becomes quite tolerable. It's a jazz instrumental with an alto sax at the forefront. It's Earl Bostic and *Harlem Nocturne*. It's the kind of music that would grace any film about the dark side of city nights – rain, fog and a barely cloaked hint of danger. It was used as the theme for one of the old *Mike Hammer* TV series. And as such was pretty near perfect in my view."

♫

"So now we reach the point where you have to make a further choice. A wave comes along and washes all your records away, but you have a chance to save just one of them. Which is it to be?"

"That really is a difficult one, Kirsty, but I'm sure all your guests say that. I think I'm going to let all the songs go. The sounds are going to be more important to me than words in this circumstance. So it's a choice between Vivaldi and Earl Bostic. Or Weather Report. It's not going to be Weather

320

Report. And I'm choosing – choosing – Vivaldi. But ask me again in half an hour and the choice might be a different one. I am changeable like that, you know. I am The Weather."

"Oh, I think we all know how quickly you can change

"You can also choose a book to have with you on your desert island. *The Bible* and the *Complete Works of Shakespeare* are already there. So what is your selection?"

"Well Kirsty, I do have my worldwide presence, as you know, but I know this programme goes out in Britain, and I think Britain is where I have my biggest fans. Many British writers have tried to describe me and define me, to predict me and prevent me, and the entire nation does seem to be completely caught up in me and everything I do. No other country in the world is like that, not even the ones where they still worship me as a god. So the book I am going to take with me is a British one. It's called *And Now the Weather*. It describes itself as *a celebration of our* (that's your) *national obsession* (which is me). I hope it will help me understand just why it is I am simultaneously so popular and so unpopular here in the UK."

"*And Now the Weather* is yours. You can also take with you a luxury – something that will be of no practical use but that will mean something to you."

"Well, this really has been the most difficult part of the exercise. As I mentioned earlier, I have no corporeal existence, so the kind of luxuries your castaways might choose will mean little to me. But, if this is a desert island, I am assuming there aren't going to be any deciduous trees there."

"I suspect you may be right."

"In that case, I would like a small wood, a coppice even, with a few sycamores or beech trees or horse chestnuts and the like, trees that shed their leaves in autumn so that, on a few occasions in the year, I can blow fallen leaves around, and get them to swirl and dance around in small spirals, in vortices. It may sound childish, perhaps even silly, but it really has been one of the things I've always enjoyed most about my role everywhere on the planet. It's the nearest I can get to playing games and relaxing."

"A small wood with a few deciduous trees – I'm sure that can be arranged. The Weather, thank you for sharing with us your Desert Island Discs."

"Thank you, Kirsty."

"Next week, listeners, we will continue this short series of non-human, abstract concept castaways when we welcome another phenomenon. Not a natural one this time, one very much man made, but one almost as far reaching in its effect on the population of the planet. Next week we will be discussing the Desert Island Discs of Austerity."